"So you've finally flipped out, have you, Jake?"

He chuckled. "I figured it was about time I came home and finally did something about you, Anne. You're thirty-one. A female bachelor, getting fussier and more set in your ways every day."

She headed for the door. "Out you go," she said cheerfully. "It's been a wonderful conversation, Jake, after not seeing you for three whole years. I won't even mention that it's two in the morning, that you had no right to pick my locks—"

"I came in through the window."

"What—?"

"Come here, Anne."

His voice was a husky, seductive tenor. A call from the north woods, a low, primitive mating call that echoed through wind and night and silence...

Dear Reader:

Romance readers today have more choice among books than ever before. But with so many titles to choose from, deciding what to select becomes increasingly difficult.

At SECOND CHANCE AT LOVE we try to make that decision easy for you — by publishing romances of the highest quality every month. You can confidently buy any SECOND CHANCE AT LOVE romance and know it will provide you with solid romantic entertainment.

Sometimes you buy romances by authors whose work you've previously read and enjoyed — which makes a lot of sense. You're being sensible . . . and careful . . . to look for satisfaction where you've found it before.

But if you're *too* careful, you risk overlooking exceptional romances by writers whose names you don't immediately recognize. These first-time authors may be the stars of tomorrow, and you won't want to miss any of their books! At SECOND CHANCE AT LOVE, many writers who were once "new" are now the most popular contributors to the line. So trying a new writer at SECOND CHANCE AT LOVE isn't really a risk at all. Every book we publish must meet our rigorous standards — whether it's by a popular "regular" or a newcomer.

In the months to come, we urge you to watch for these names — Linda Raye, Karen Keast, Betsy Osborne, Dana Daniels, and Cinda Richards. All are dazzling new writers, an elite few whose books are destined to become "keepers." We think you'll be delighted and excited by their first books with us!

Look, too, for romances by writers with whom you're already warmly familiar: Jeanne Grant, Ann Cristy, Linda Barlow, Elissa Curry, Jan Mathews, and Liz Grady, among many others.

Best wishes,

Ellen Edwards

Ellen Edwards, Senior Editor
SECOND CHANCE AT LOVE
The Berkley Publishing Group
200 Madison Avenue
New York, N.Y. 10016

SILVER
AND SPICE

JEANNE GRANT

SECOND CHANCE AT LOVE
BOOK

Other books by
Jeanne Grant

Second Chance at Love
MAN FROM TENNESSEE #49
A DARING PROPOSITION #149
KISSES FROM HEAVEN #167
WINTERGREEN #184

To Have and to Hold
SUNBURST #14
TROUBLE IN PARADISE #28

SILVER AND SPICE

First edition published October 1984

First printing

"Second Chance at Love" and the butterfly emblem are trademarks belonging to Jove Publications, Inc.

Printed in the United States of America

Second Chance at Love books are published by
The Berkley Publishing Group
200 Madison Avenue, New York, NY 10016

chapter 1

ANNE WAS RESTLESS.

Just behind her, hothousé orchids festooned the curved mahogany banister. As she wandered outside onto the Cords' terrace, she saw a trio of musicians playing Haydn, their foreheads glistening beneath Japanese lanterns. On the lawn by the pool, four long tables, draped in Irish linen, were laden with gourmet fare. Oysters, raw. Sautéed frogs' legs. Crackers heaped with Russian caviar. The little black blobs were mounded high, Anne noted wryly. A *bit* of caviar denied the true taste; a *mound* delivered the appropriate experience. Tuxedoed waiters circulated between house and yard bearing trays of champagne in hollow-stemmed glasses. Anne considered dryly that Loretta Cord's "only a simple Sunday barbecue, darling" had been rather an understatement.

She shouldn't have come, Anne told herself as she went back into the house. Many nights she might have enjoyed the Cords' gala, but tonight wasn't one of them. Tonight she was in a strange mood; she felt like taking a midnight walk in her bare feet when the rain was pelting down, for instance. Knowing she wasn't the walk-in-the-

1

rain type made her feel even more irritable. And because she was rarely so out of sorts, she felt triply annoyed with herself.

She knew why Loretta had invited her. Oh, Link— the sweetheart—had undoubtedly been the one to propose her name for the guest list, but subject, of course, to his wife's approval. And Loretta, naturally, *had* approved. Yes, Loretta Cord knew that a banker is a wonderful friend to have when one's mink isn't paid for. Actually, Loretta's mink had been paid for, but the lady always covered her bets.

Others at the party had not been so clever through the recession. Certain pairs of eyes shifted from Anne's as she wandered from room to room. It always happened. As a trust officer, Anne really didn't know or care whether anyone regularly overdrew his or her checking account, but people assumed she was privy to all their financial transactions and reacted instinctively. When one saw a police car in the rearview mirror, one slowed down to the legal speed. When a priest wandered by, one stopped screaming at Jimmy and kissed the little monster. And when a banker ambled into the vicinity, one miraculously remembered every financial misdemeanor of one's life.

Taking a sip from her first glass of champagne, Anne knew that she could make the effort, transcend the touchy social barriers, and even have a good time. These were neighbors if not close friends, and moodiness really wasn't her scene. It was just tonight . . . She sighed and continued to prowl restlessly through the Cords' spacious house, which was mansion even by Grosse Pointe standards.

She caught a glimpse of herself in a hallway mirror and frowned broodingly. Her ash-blond hair was waist length; tonight, as always, it was appropriately roped, tied, and tamed with pins. Her back was covered only by a latticework of black raw silk that seemed more bare space than fabric, though in front the gown demurely stretched to a high-banded collar. Well, perhaps "demurely" was not precisely accurate. The bias cut in front very definitely emphasized her pert, rounded breasts, unremarkable in size but rather sassily uptilted. At the waist, the gown gave up teasing and simply fell to the floor. As she strolled the length of the hallway, a slit in the dress revealed a slim long calf and thigh.

Nature had endowed her with vulnerable, deep-set eyes of a soft green, heavily lashed and accented with slim, arched brows. Nature had also bestowed on her a cameo-fragile complexion, high, delicate cheekbones, a nose just a little too long, and distinctly shaped, petal-soft lips.

Anne had never been grateful for nature's gifts, however. She had chased the vulnerable look from her eyes with subtle gray eye shadow; she had used foundation and blusher to make her skin seem less fragile; and she had expertly lined her delicate mouth with lip pencil and then gloss. She'd learned a long time ago to make a little makeup go a long way. Overall the image was flawless, aristocratic—an image Anne expected of herself. She had hidden all of her natural touch-me looks inside a not-to-be-touched perfection.

Exactly the goal.

With a sigh, Anne strolled into the living room to join the other party guests, determined to shake herself out of the brooding mood. She was talking to Blaire Culverton when she saw *him* . . . the wolfish profile and sand-silver hair, pagan shoulders stifled in a black tux. He had his arm around a little brunette with beautiful, straight white teeth. He kissed the woman lightly, laughing . . . and—for no reason that Anne could tell—looked up.

His eyes captured hers before she could look away. Silvery-gray eyes, predatory eyes. They shifted slowly up and down the black silk dress, the carefully applied makeup and the well-constrained hair; just as slowly, a crooked half-smile appeared at the corners of his mouth. Anne could guess the picture he had conjured up in his mind, of each layer of perfection peeled away at the slow, lazy pace that would suit him. His jaw firmed as the smile suddenly left his mouth and the wolfish eyes met hers again and his gaze bored into her. The message was starkly sexual, not a playful come-on or invitation, but a bold claim of possession. *I'm going to have you...*

Don't hold your breath, she thought fleetingly, but her face went pale. Not that she couldn't hold her own with a wolf here and there. She was thirty-one, no child. Yet her palms were oddly cold and damp, her throat ridiculously dry. And her heart was beating a mad tattoo...

She put an arm on Blaire's shoulder and stood on tiptoe to kiss his cheek, murmuring an apology for having to leave the arresting conversation on supply-side economics. In a graceful swirl of black silk, she deliberately wended her way out of the living room and into the hall, near the banister with the orchids. There were people there, lots and lots of people...

"Anne? Darling, I haven't seen you in so long!" In a cloud of Shalimar and rose chiffon, Jane Harrison gathered up Anne for a buss and a hug. The two women laughed and settled on the third step of the long stairway. "I'm *so* glad to see you after all this time!" Jane exclaimed. "I've got all sorts of things to tell you..."

The caterers were even willing to deliver champagne to stair-sitters, and Jane Harrison had the same sort of effervescence as the sparkling wine. Their friendship had initially been created by sharing any number of totally erroneous concepts about love, life, and sex—late at night over potato chips—at the private high school they'd both attended. After fifteen years, Jane was still the talker—*her* children, *her* interests, *her* divorce—while Anne still listened, not unhappy to dole out numerous affectionate servings of compassion, as long as Jane didn't expect her to bare her own soul. But Jane certainly never did that, so gradually Anne felt her limbs relax again, her pulse obediently slow as Jane chattered.

Twenty minutes lapsed, full of laughter and old memories, before another tray of champagne lilted past and Jane rose and stepped forward to retrieve fresh glasses for the two of them. From behind Anne, out of nowhere, she felt a shivery touch at the nape of her neck.

Jane turned around, her blue eyes widening as she took in the retreating figure in black tux. When he was out of sight, she grinned impishly at Anne, setting down both champagne glasses. "Did you see that hunk?" she whispered appreciatively, sighing as she refolded the rose chiffon over her chunky legs. "Wonder what he was doing upstairs?" she added with a wicked little smile. "You don't know him, do you? What's the matter, darling?"

"*Nothing.* Oh, of all the ridiculous . . . I seem to have lost some hairpins."

They both searched. Nothing remotely resembling a hairpin was anywhere near the stairs. With a smile, Anne cut off the conversation with Jane and maneuvered quickly down the hall to a bathroom. Apprehensively, she forced herself to look in the mirror. The loss of a half-dozen hairpins made a difference to a mane of hair that reached her waist. The style, rearranged, was of necessity less severe, with looser loops and curls that were not anywhere near as . . . perfect.

She'd taken merely four steps into the living room when she realized that *he* was there. This time he was talking to a cluster of men, his tux jacket open and one of his hands loosely in a pocket as he laughed. The strong features and silvery eyes again reminded her of a wolf. On the endangered species list in many parts of the world, wolves. Anne, normally sympathetic to that cause, couldn't seem to raise any compassion. He managed to turn toward her before she could back up and out of sight.

His silver eyes were steely with determination. The intent to stalk his prey was so blatant that she caught her breath. And then lifted her chin, turning away with a small smile. The poor man was so arrogant. But just how far did he think he could take his little game in a houseful of people?

She wanted air, anyway. On the terrace, dancers were cuddled up for the torch songs the musicians were now playing. A restless breeze ruffled the white tablecloths on the lawn by the pool; lanterns swayed in the cloudy September night. A very nice, very safe man caught her eye . . .

She'd occasionally dated Warren Stuart summers, or on college semester breaks. He'd earned his law degree at Harvard since then, and as if his body knew it, he wasn't nearly as good a dancer as he'd once been. The stiffness lingered even as he tried to hold her close, undoubtedly hoping to forget his wife and two children. So much for safety. Still, Anne closed her eyes, the picture of a lady enjoying herself, caught up in the music and the night and a good-looking man. The slight breeze cooled the unaccustomed color in her cheeks.

Her fingers curled loosely over Warren's collar, as his did at her waist. He pulled back, smiling at her. "You always were the best, Anne," he said warmly. "I haven't seen you in so long. Happy these days?"

She nodded simply, and he pulled her close again. The patio around them grew crowded, making it more and more difficult to dance without bumping into someone. When the last chords of the second song died, she drew back from Warren, smiling. "You think we've been at it long enough to make your wife jealous?" she asked teasingly.

He laughed, throwing back his head. "If it weren't for Amanda, honey . . ."

Warren's hands were affectionately holding hers, yet like the caress of a breeze she again felt the shiver of fingertips behind her. It was nothing. Just the merest touch at the base of her neck, and then the swift sweep of a hand all the way down to the intimate curve of her hips. Undoubtedly an accident—someone trying to move past the crowd of dancers. Of course. Her smile never faltered, but her hand whipped out of Warren's, her fingers instinctively closing around the nape of her neck as if she'd suddenly discovered an aching muscle. "I'm going to have a little talk with your Amanda," she told

Warren with a little laugh before leaving him and swiftly making her way off the patio.

Unfortunately, both bathrooms on the ground floor were occupied. Belatedly, she remembered a small one off the kitchen, and smiled apologetically at the harried catering crew filling up trays as she passed. In the tiny square cubicle, she hurriedly refastened the collar that held up her dress. If she had been any less quick, her breasts would have been on display. *Not* Anne's style.

There was a million-to-one chance, of course, that the two hooks and eyes had loosened on their own. Most people, she knew, would probably never even notice his resemblance to a wolf. Most people would probably be totally taken in by the character lines etched deeply between the man's brows, around his mouth and eyes. A character made up of humor and certainly intelligence and whatever wayward charm had led a group of conservative, prominent men to cluster around him . . . no one but Anne would have guessed that he was capable of such a *childish,* unforgivable, ridiculous, arrogant . . .

Anne glanced at the mirror and was taken aback at the sight of her luminous jade-green eyes so unconsciously full of laughter. The devil!

Hurriedly, she slipped back to join the party, this time deliberately seeking her host. She found Link Cord near the pool filling his plate, his wife at his side. Link was sixty, gray-haired, and husky, these days sporting iron-gray whiskers that were supposed to look distinguished . . . and in any case hid a smoothly rounded chin. To Anne, he still very much resembled the neighbor she remembered from childhood—the man who had filled her pockets with silver dollars the day she'd dropped an ice cream cone on the grass, a long time ago. And when he saw her, his dark blue eyes sparkled, the corners crinkling like tiny fans. He opened his arms, and she willingly snuggled into them.

"I was beginning to wonder if you were here, sweetheart. I didn't see you."

"I've been here and having a marvelous time," Anne assured him, and then hugged Loretta Cord as well, with a little less enthusiasm. "You've done it all exactly right, as always," she whispered to Link.

He was sensitive about that. Link had come from some rustic cow town in Nebraska, and the exact amount of caviar on each cracker was a critical matter to him, thanks to years of lectures from Loretta. He beamed down at Anne. "Come on, come on. We'll get you something to eat. And don't give me any nonsense about your figure. You've got everyone in the place outclassed and you know it . . ."

Obediently, Anne filled up her plate with oysters and crab and frogs' legs she had no intention of eating, and edged away just a little so that Link and Loretta could greet another guest.

From the corner of her eye, she saw *him* again. He was dancing, his partner a tall, sylphlike woman with a spectacular head of red hair. A lovely woman, really . . .

The silver-gray eyes met hers. Did he actually understand that once she'd paid her respects to the Cords she was free to leave? The man seemed to have no manners at all, deserting his redhead in the middle of a dance. Rapidly, Anne averted her eyes and frantically searched for a place to set her plate down. The game was fun, but the thought of an actual meeting caused panic to well up inside her.

He was moving slowly toward her, enjoying the stalk. Behind her host's back, Anne set her plate down, took a single quick step, and felt Link's hand curl around her wrist like a velvet handcuff. "Come on, sweetheart," he whispered. "There's someone I've been wanting you to meet for a long time."

With Link hugging her shoulder, Anne turned, smiling weakly as she stared with deliberate disinterest at a chin made of steel. Just a small distance up from that chin was a disconcertingly sensual mouth, curved in a half-mocking smile. "Anne Blake, is it?" She had to lift her head to meet his gaze. He had the advantage of looking down, his silvery eyes hooded for Link's benefit. Not for hers. He was staring at her mouth, as if the only thing on his mind was crushing it ... very softly, very thoroughly.

"This is Jake Rivard, Anne. I never did understand how the two of you never happened to meet up before," Link said jovially. "Heck, you both had parents that hopped the globe, but your grandparents lived just three doors away from each other. And in the last few years Anne's even done business for your grandfather, Jake."

"Mr ... Rivers?"

He took the hand she had not extended, chuckling appreciatively at her deliberate mistake. "Rivard," he corrected lazily. "Fine party, Link."

"I noticed you were having a good time, Jake," Link said with satisfaction.

Anne had also noticed that Jake was enjoying himself. First with the brunette, and then with the redhead. And he was still having a good time, imprisoning her small hand neatly in his larger one. She could feel the grain of calluses on his palm, and she could also feel her control begin to slip, the control she always resented losing. The stalk had been going on for more than an hour. Her humor was beginning to give way to an attack of nerves. A delicious adrenaline was coursing through her bloodstream; she was well aware of the danger. She felt high, light-headed. He was a powerful sexual animal. She valued that in the same way that she respected any predator—as long as he understood that she wasn't prey.

His hand slowly freed hers, his thumb gently rubbing against her slender wrist as he let her go. "You don't mind if I take Anne away for a dance, do you, Link?"

"Of course not. You just show her a real good time, Jake. She's one special lady to me."

Anne smiled weakly. "Actually, I sort of left a friend all alone in the house. If you would mind just for a moment, Mr.—"

"Rivard," he supplied.

"I'll be right back to claim that dance," she assured him.

"I'm sure you will."

There would be a snowstorm in hell before her cool, calm flesh would come in direct contact with his lean, hungry body—and he knew it. She could feel his eyes on the open spaces in the back of her dress as she walked away.

It didn't matter. Anne was leaving. Well, in a minute she was leaving. She wanted to see one last person before she left.

Angela Stone was a white-haired wisp of an aristocrat, dressed in a plain white gown with a blaze of sapphires at her throat. "How's your grandmother, Anne? I spoke to her on the phone last week, but neither of us really had a chance to talk..."

Anne tried to relax, taking the straight chair next to the older woman. "I miss her when she goes south," Anne admitted. "In fact, I've been worried about her lately."

"Now, she has a horde of people to take care of her, dear. You're so very like her, Anne, never letting anyone do a thing for you. One doesn't quibble with that kind of character; one simply tries to relax and not worry. Tell me what you've been up to."

Anne automatically shied from talking about herself. Instead, she switched to Mrs. Stone's favorite subject—her artists and the scholarships she'd set up for budding sculptors. Occasionally, people came by to interrupt; Link, for one, bent over to kiss Angela's cheek, and another neighbor did the same to Anne. The later it grew, the cooler the breeze became, and more and more people wandered inside. Still, it wasn't until Anne felt a curl start to slip on her neck that she realized he'd been there again.

With a flush in her cheeks, she stood up—but not soon enough. She could feel all the snaky coils of long hair begin to unwind. "I'll tell Gran everything you said,

Mrs. Stone. How good it is to see you again."

"So few people take the time for an old lady these days, Anne. Give Jennie my love."

Anne managed to reach the front door before her hair actually tumbled. She reached up frantically; there were three pins left. Irritably, she wrenched those out, and the rest of the tumbling mane promptly cascaded down her back, all soft and tickly through the silk latticework of her dress.

It didn't matter; she was through with the party anyway. From the front steps, she could see the long line of cars parked along the road; the cement walk that led down to them was bordered by hedges trimmed into animal shapes. One bush was a wolf. The long slope of grass had the sheen of dew; fall leaves whispered as she hurried through the darkness toward the shores of Lake St. Clair. She had parked her car a block away.

As she approached her little red MG, her step faltered. He was already there, leaning back against the car directly ahead of hers. The dark green Morgan had not been there when she parked; her MG had barely fit between two monstrous gas guzzlers, and she remembered both well. His sleek car was of classic vintage, long and low, not the type of car she was likely to forget.

He was leaning back, arms folded lazily across his chest. Even in the darkness, she could make out the silvery eyes, glinting directly on hers, the waiting in them controlled. Barely. Impatiently, she reached her car, leaned over to toss in her purse, and then, with exasperation, slipped off one shoe and hurled it at him. Then the other. He was picking up the silver sandals when she vaulted into the driver's seat, hitching up her skirts in a motion that proved she had given up on ladylike modesty.

Her stockinged toe pressed lightly on the accelerator as she started the engine, and with practiced finesse she edged the MG rapidly out of the parking space. In seconds, she was roaring down the quiet boulevard, her long hair spinning a cloak around her. She saw from her rearview mirror that he hadn't even gotten in his car yet.

During the fifteen-minute drive to her condominium, nearly all of Anne's image of perfection was destroyed. Her stockings were snagged, her skirt was hitched up over her knees, her hair was a witch's tangle around her, she'd bitten off the shiny lip gloss, and the wind had whipped away most of her other makeup. She was exceeding the speed limit, so she hugged the dark side roads where no one was likely to notice her. The police had little to do in this affluent suburb of Detroit except catch speeders.

Braking sharply as she reached her condo, Anne felt a moment of triumph when she saw that there wasn't another car in sight. Certainly not a long, low Morgan. Holding her skirts up, she sprinted over the wet, grassy yard to reach her door, breathless as she worked the key in the lock.

In seconds, she was inside and throwing the deadbolt, and then she leaned back against the door until she could breathe normally again. Every nerve ending was tingling. Laughter was trying to bubble up inside of her.

The condo was dark, with only the pale light from the small lamp falling on the pair of white velvet couches with their scattering of shocking pink pillows. Her fig tree was getting huge, playing a marvelous game of Shadows on the thick white carpet. The chrome and pewter appointments gleamed, giving evidence of her meticulous care; magazines were neatly aligned on small, elegant tables. Somewhere along the way she seemed to have accumulated a collection of marble eggs; their pearly pink surfaces shone from the far corner of the French bookcase. Everything was in its place, all feminine perfection. She loved the look of the room.

Usually.

Switching off the small lamp, Anne ran her fingers back through her hair with a little sigh. A desperate feeling of disappointment came from nowhere to clutch at her heart. The chase had set off a confused kaleidoscope of emotions, none of which she wanted to deal with. Taking a brush from her purse, she restored at least basic order to her hair as she wandered into the kitchen. Thirsty suddenly, she took a long drink of water and listened, for a moment, to the lonely silence. A neighbor's light went off in the distance across the courtyard, the only other light that had been on besides her own.

Slowly, she made her way to the bedroom and pushed open the door.

He was there. Lying back against her pillows, his shoes off and the tux jacket opened, his unbuttoned shirt baring several inches of that sand-silver mat of hair on his chest.

Her heart skipped two beats and then raced; a small fist clenched in the folds of her skirt. "To begin with, there isn't any *possible* way you could have gotten here ahead of me, and don't even *tell* me how you got in," she said furiously. "And to end with, Jake, the answer is *no. Not again. Not this time.*"

"Now, Anne." His tone was coaxing, lazy. Slowly, he swung his legs over the side of her bed, taking three long strides before he reached her, her silver sandals dangling by their straps from one finger. "You didn't really think the deadbolt would keep me out?" The gun metal left his eyes; pewter-softened, they took in, correctly, that odd blend of vulnerability and stubborn determination that was Anne. "I've come better than two thousand miles to tell you I think it's about time we got married," he told her. "Let's not start off with a quarrel."

chapter 2

ANNE HEARD HIM; she even had a vagrant urge to try a swinging left hook to wipe the uneven grin off his face. For one helpless moment, though, she couldn't stop herself from making a quick, fierce study of the man. Her eyes swept over the familiar planes of Jake's face, resenting the new, unexplained crease between his brows, scanning the hook nose and sensual mouth and the chin so inevitably peppered with evening stubble. If there had been the least sign that he had been ill over the last three years; if by any chance he had been ill and she hadn't known...Jake was such a terrible fool when it came to taking care of himself.

About the instant her eyes were finally reassured that he was perfectly fine, she was uncomfortably aware that the devilish spark in his own eyes had increased to a full-fledged flame. Clearly, he was delighted by whatever emotions her transparent face had given away. And about that same instant, the word "married" finally registered in her brain like the surprise little bomb that it was.

"Married?" she echoed lightly. Her vulnerable eyes turned cool, and her tone deliberately radiated solici-

15

ousness. "So you've finally flipped out, have you, Jake?"

He chuckled as he handed her the sandals. She wasted
no time putting them on. His hand on her shoulder was
undoubtedly intended to offer her balance . . . except that
the feel of that hand threw her *off* balance. Behind all
the lazy laughter in his eyes was a stark, steady glint of
determination. "Now, don't get scared," he said teasingly.

"Scared?"

"Like the little girl who's lying in bed waiting for the
alligators under the mattress to come and get her. Marriage doesn't have to be like that, honey." Absently, Jake
pushed the hair back from his forehead, a gesture that
failed to restore order of any kind. "I figured it was about
time I came home and finally did something about you,
Anne. You're thirty-one. A female bachelor, getting
fussier and more set in your ways every day. Pretty soon
you'll be over the hill—"

"True." She added with a remarkable amount of compassion, "Perhaps age is your problem, too? Maybe you're
going through a midlife crisis, Jake. I think you can get
pills for that."

"Not until I'm forty; I still have six years to go. Speaking of pills, are you taking any?"

"Brewer's yeast," she said sweetly. "And occasionally
wheat germ."

Damn that crooked smile of his. It was the sexy eyes
that had initially led her down the primrose path to his
bed a very long time ago, but it was the impossibly
crooked smile that had made her fall in love with him.
Memories flooded her consciousness as if a dam had
burst.

She plugged the hole in the dike and headed for the door.
"Out you go," she said cheerfully. "It's been a wonderful
conversation, Jake, after not seeing you for three whole
years. I won't even mention that it's two in the morning,
that you had no right to pick my locks—"

"Window."

"Pardon?"

"I came in through the window."

"What—?" But it was obvious which window he had come in—the one near the bed where the curtains were fluttering in the night breeze. Anne found herself staring, suddenly lost. Jake had climbed in another window another time, when she was eighteen. And made love and made love and made love and . . . She lifted her face to his, jade eyes turned emerald. "Go away, Jake. Just go completely away."

"Now, Anne." Jake's hand brushed the small of her back as he urged her through the door. "You know we're both dying for a cup of coffee."

"You are *not* staying."

"Of course not."

Despite the seeming meekness of his tone, Jake's words echoed in the hall with the reverberation of a detonated grenade. Anne had waged war with Jake before. She wavered momentarily, weighing the dangers of spending fifteen minutes with Jake over a cup of coffee in the same way a general might calculate the risk of sending his troops over a mine field. A good general, of course, would send the troops *around* the mine field.

Anne let out a breath. "One cup of coffee," she said flatly. "Only so you can tell me what trouble you've gotten yourself into the last few years."

"Lots," he assured her. His slashed-on smile was her reward. Jake always rewarded terrible judgment.

Her unwilling heart turned a cartwheel. Her heart had turned cartwheels for those special private smiles three other times in her life—not counting that first time Jake had loved her and left her, when she was eighteen and he twenty-one. "I'll just bet you have," she said lightly. "So where have you been raising hell this time?"

"Idaho. Northern Idaho, where the mountains are so steep they can barely build roads. Where the whole area's deserted. You can walk for hours and have the feeling no one has ever been there before you."

"Sounds perfectly dreadful." They fell into old habits in the kitchen. Jake opened cupboards and drawers, finally finding the instant coffee and cups.

"A minute," she told him when the cups were filled and he was staring at the dials on her microwave oven.

He punched the button. "This is nicer than your last place."

"I like it," she agreed, trailing after him with spoons, place mats, napkins, cream in a sterling pitcher, and a matching sugar bowl. All the things she considered appropriate for serving coffee, knowing full well Jake would have been content to sit near a campfire with a mug.

"It's nicer . . . but the kitchen's still just like you. Your grandmother's hand-painted china and everything in its place, all the cups lined up just so."

"I'm the same old frantic neatnik," Anne agreed. "So how long have you been back in town?" she asked casually.

"Since late this afternoon. Just long enough to find out where you were, pick up the Morgan from Gramps, and get to Link's party." He set both cups on the table, but didn't seem interested in drinking from his own. He was still trying to undress. Not that Anne didn't understand that Jake had an honest antipathy for formal attire, but one could stretch understanding only so far. His shoes and tie had been off when she came in; somehow the jacket was off now. Jake was looking very, very comfortable as he leaned back against the counter, his shirt cuffs folded back, the silver hair on his chest showing in the V of his open shirt. All settled in. He had the wolf's ability to move slowly and lazily when he was clearly up to no good.

Anne settled in a chair and lifted her coffee cup. "Either you heave your suitcase out the back door onto the porch, or I will," she said pleasantly.

He chuckled. "Did you get all the presents I sent you?"

"I mean it. You can't just come back here—"

"In a minute, Anne. Meanwhile, what on earth are you doing living alone?" Jake asked conversationally.

"The same thing you are. Being very happy in my own way."

"I counted at least twelve men at the party who would have been happy to convince you otherwise."

"Thirteen," she said mildly. Her palms curled around the warm cup, suddenly needing that warmth. "I only counted one brunette and one redhead in your corner, but then you weren't there more than an hour. Either one, I'm sure, will be happy to store your suitcase for you for the night."

"Come here, Anne."

His voice was a husky, seductive tenor. A call from the north woods, a low, primitive mating call that echoed through wind and night and silence...and had nothing at all to do with a brightly lit, spotless kitchen in an affluent suburb. A drop of coffee splashed on Anne's wrist as she set down her cup and stood up.

"All right. *I'll* put your suitcase on the porch," she said reasonably.

She moved swiftly, so swiftly that she almost made it to the doorway before his fingers curled around her wrist and tugged, very gently. Just as gently, the rest of the room suddenly went out of focus. Her meticulous kitchen with its bright porcelains and immaculate chrome all blurred; Jake's face was the only thing in focus. She took in the fan of character lines around his eyes and the grainy texture of his sun-weathered skin, the shaggy brows...A helpless murmur escaped her throat as his lips touched hers, once, soothingly, his mouth soft and smooth, the taste of him something she'd never been able to forget. "God, I've missed you, Anne. God, I've missed you..."

Her hands hung limply at her sides as she fought the rush of a thousand memories. The smell of Jake, the look of the long, curling hairs on his chest, his Adam's apple and the cords of his neck, the feel of being wrapped up in a world of senses where nothing else mattered...His fingers combed back her hair, clenching and unclenching in the long, silken strands as they had done so many times before.

Their relationship had never worked, and never would

work except on this one level. She knew that far too
well, far too painfully...but his lips were so warm,
brushing over and over on hers until they trembled, until
they parted and his mouth molded itself to hers and his
tongue slipped inside. God, she'd missed him. No one
had ever even come close to filling the emptiness but
Jake. Love, hate, frustration, laughter, and sheer wild
passion...a thousand emotions were involved in her
feelings for her roguish wolf, only half of them pleasant,
none of them comfortable, not one of them having the
least thing to do with the well-ordered life she took such
pride and satisfaction in.

No, Anne, moaned her very rational brain, which was
an expert on survival. Her hands refused to listen, slowly
running up his arms, reexploring the mold of his shoulder
muscles before she allowed her fingers to curl up in his
thick, springy hair. Some of the tension left his body
when he felt her acquiesce; his lips again softened on
hers.

"I'm never leaving without you again," he murmured.
"Hear me, Anne, because you're going with me..."

She couldn't hear anything; in a resounding rush, her
heart was pounding out a song she'd heard many
times...but never with this particular chorus. Never
with this particular need to force his lips back to hers,
this ache for the claim of his hand on her breast, this
fierce resentment of the intrusion of clothes. She'd thought
she would never see him again. The last time, she'd told
him never to come back, and meant it. Jake *knew* she'd
meant it. Only now, like a crocus bursting through snow,
she felt vulnerable and full of life again and reaching for
sunlight and desperately unwilling to let go even for a
moment...

"So sweet," he whispered. "So sweet, Anne."

His lips dipped into the hollow of her neck and his
breath tickled her throat, warm and whispery. His thighs
rubbed against hers in an evocative dance. Every movement he made increased the rush of sensations in her
body, even his evening beard that chafed like crushed

velvet against her soft skin. His hands swept up and down her spine as he trailed haunting slow kisses along the side of her neck. When his lips sought hers again, she was waiting. The pressure she returned was wanton, her fingers raking up through his hair, a fierce, racing, desperate cry of need escaping from her. How she loved this man! How she had longed for the look of him, for his touch and smell and sound and taste ... She could feel his pleasure at her ardent response as intimately as she could feel the unmistakable pressure of his arousal against her abdomen. She'd denied her loneliness for so long ... too long.

A flush of heat touched her cheeks as his eyes met hers, all silver, all pagan shine. Far too slowly, he wrapped his fingers in her hair to nudge the strands aside. His knuckles grazed the nape of her neck as he sought the hooks at the back of her gown. In a moment, she was naked to the waist.

The next moment he had gathered her so close that neither of them could breathe. Her arms locked around his neck; her lips burrowed in his throat. "This time," he whispered fiercely, "you're going to marry me, Anne. This time the ball's in my court ..."

Marry ... the word stung like a lash of a whip. Her passion chilled with lightning speed. Shaking, Anne jerked back from him, snatching for the front of her gown. *"Dammit,* Jake ..." Normally it took two fingers to handle the hooks and eyes; now she seemed to have ninety and still couldn't manage it. "Damn *you."* She held the gown up with one hand. Feeling sick and furious, she could barely look him in the eyes. *"You* started that. You know I never meant to—"

"Yes," he said shortly, and tugged her trembling cheek to his ruffled shirt front, managing the hooks and eyes himself. When he stepped back from her, he was oddly still, his body radiating none of the tension and frustration that were pulsating through her own. The watchful look in his eyes was unfamiliar, like a terrible new trick, as if he could read her faint trembling, her pale color and porcelain profile, and see things . . . that just weren't there.

"Look, I don't find the subject of marriage very amusing."

"It wasn't meant to be."

"It won't *work,*" she said furiously. "And you know that just as well as I do!"

"It *will* work."

Be calm. Anne took a breath and then another, staring in total frustration at the ceiling. "Even you, Jake, cannot expect to just walk in here after three years and—"

"And talk marriage? But I just have, Anne. Because we know each other far too well to pretend time has made any difference. You know it hasn't." He reached out, and the pad of his thumb very gently caressed her cheek, a touch as tender as the look in his eyes was determined. "We just proved that," he said roughly. "We've always proved that, every time we touch each other."

"You think you deserve a gold medal because I still want you?" she demanded. "*Rabbits* want each other, Jake. You want to hear me say that I missed you? Well, fine. I missed you like hell. And now you can just get the devil out of here."

Enough was enough. Actually, enough was just past enough, because she could feel an unfamiliar, disgraceful welling of moisture in her eyes. Anne never cried. Turning on her heel, she stalked toward her room.

Jake didn't follow. In seconds, she'd turned the lock on her bedroom door and leaned back against it, her arms wrapped around her chest, her eyes closed. Waiting for Jake to go.

Moments later, she heard sounds from the other room, but definitely not the sound of the front door closing. It took her five minutes to realize that instead of leaving, he was actually . . . settling in for the night! She tried to decide whether her fragile poise was up to going back out there and forcing the issue.

Finally moving away from the door, she slowly took off her dress and hung it in the closet. Then she slipped

on a long flannel nightgown. Even when the light was
off and the comforter up to her chin, she found herself
staring at the door in the darkness, waiting for the knob
to turn. It didn't. Eventually, the light under the door
went out. If you had a whit of sense you would call the
police, a small voice in her head advised.

The thought brought an exhausted though definite hint
of a smile to her face. That kind of flamboyant gesture
was certainly not her style. Besides, there was no con-
ceivable reason she shouldn't offer an old friend her
couch for the night. And Jake had once been an old
friend, an old childhood friend, before they became lovers.

The gold hands on the alarm clock announced 5:07
A.M. An ungodly hour to find oneself staring at the ceiling. Anne finally gave up trying to sleep and threw off
the covers. Gathering up underthings from her drawers,
she silently unlocked her door and tiptoed out.

Jake was asleep, sprawled on the carpet in the living
room. She might have guessed he'd find her couch too
confining. He'd found the blankets in the bathroom closet,
but his chest and one long leg were uncovered. Jake was
out like a light, his silvery hair thick and disheveled on
the pillow. Biting her lip at the oddly vulnerable look of
him, she tiptoed into the bathroom and flipped on the
light, then closed the door.

A stranger sleepily confronted her in the mirror, a
wanton mermaid with hair streaming over her breasts, a
Lorelei with stormy green eyes and plum-swollen lips . . .
a moral degenerate who'd come close to selling her soul
in the middle of the night to have that man share the
pillow with her.

She turned her back on Lorelei, peeled off her nightgown and put on a stark white bra and simple bikini
underpants. Carefully, she fitted her pantyhose to her
long, sleek legs; she snapped the waistband in place with
a vengeance.

She pulled on a plain white slip, then mercilessly

applied a brush to her hair. It took ten minutes before the long strands were completely untangled, then another five to pin a figure eight at the nape of her neck. Every strand of ash-blond hair was subdued.

Makeup came next. It wasn't quite so difficult to face the mirror; Wanton Wanda was fast being replaced by prim and proper Anne. Moisturizer, then foundation . . . She and Jake had grown up together in a way. Their grandparents had lived just three doors away from each other, grandparents whom they frequently visited as children and who, by different twists of fate, became their guardians in later years. The friendship had started when Anne was three, wailing her angelic little head off the day she fell off a tricycle. Jake, then six, had vaulted over the forbidden high fences between yards to discover the source of the caterwauling. He'd fixed the trike pedal so a giant couldn't reach it and was very proud of himself.

Jake was her dark prince from then on. Not that he didn't have the coloring to be the regular kind of prince, but Jake was clearly never cut out to wear white and ride a white steed. The *real* Prince Charming would never have gone in for an occasional game of kickball and a lot of swinging on fences and kicking stones at the lakeshore. Jake was capable of merciless teasing, and though Anne was a quiet listener with everyone else in her life, with Jake, she could never seem to stop talking. He was always listening to things she didn't want anyone to know.

Her father had died when she was five, a major blow to a scrawny little waif with green eyes. Her mother proceeded to search the whole world for another husband, and she found three before Anne reached her early teens. Their lifestyle never lacked the label "advantaged." Anne, oversensitive and painfully shy, barely survived it.

But you were hardly much of a survivor then, she told her reflection in the mirror, and she brushed faint brown eye shadow on her lids and added an almost imperceptible stroke of eyebrow pencil. Jake's childhood, like hers, had involved a great deal of travel. His parents simply liked to take to the road. They had a little Cessna . . . and the plane went down. It happened the year Jake was ten, the same year his grandfather, Gil, had taken him in, the same year he'd managed to run all the way to Tucson before the police caught up with him. Reaction to his parents' death, the neighbors clucked. Anne knew far better. Jake was born with wanderlust in his soul.

By the time she was eighteen, Anne had long been a permanent resident at her paternal grandmother's. Anne's mother had never objected to the relationship between Anne and Jennie. Children were a nuisance. Buffeted too long by fierce, painful, endless winds, Anne was still in shock; her mother had died of pneumonia two weeks earlier. She hadn't even known her mother was ill. And Jake could not possibly have known; yet he climbed in at the window of her grandmother's house to comfort her... and he made love to her. *Any* judge would have sentenced Jake harshly for taking an innocent in a weak moment. Judges knew nothing; Anne couldn't have survived that moment in her life without Jake. Two weeks later, Jake had a choice between completing his last year at Harvard and embarking on a fishing venture off the coast of Alaska. Why risk graduating with honors? Alaska had won hands down.

Anne whisked blusher on her cheeks. When he'd left she'd felt as if a jagged rock had been torn from her heart. He'd asked her to go with him on that venture. Run off to Alaska at eighteen? No. But her refusal didn't prevent her from being out of her mind in love with him, nor did it ease the desperate loneliness when he was gone.

Judging from the state of his jeans the next time she saw him, he must have blown his parents' inheritance in one quick fling. Oil-bearing shale in Montana, was it? Anne was twenty-two, graduating from college, invincible. No one could tell her otherwise. Independence and control and self-sufficiency were her goals; any number of male undergraduates had been foolish enough to try to distract her from those goals. Jake had come back out of the blue and listened as she expounded her philosophy of never needing anyone, as she told him how she would

never be vulnerable again. He'd listened, all the way to
bed, for almost two solid months.

That affair had left her bruised and worse, because
they'd fought terribly at the end. He wanted her to go
with him. She wanted him to stay. He'd split for Tulsa,
something to do with telecommunications. For months,
she saw his face in every crowd, jumped every time the
phone rang . . . But by the age of twenty-four, she was
completely over him. Completely. Serious about banking
by then, involved, busy, her own woman. She was home
with the flu the day he walked in. No doctor would have
forced her to stay in bed as long as he did. The hours
went far too swiftly; they couldn't even spare the time
to argue . . .

Anne washed her hands, switched off the light, and
tiptoed back to her bedroom. The faintest gray dawn light
was coming in at the windows. She switched on the closet
light and pulled a mauve blouse from its hanger. The
fabric was silky to the touch but totally plain, with a
stand-up collar and long sleeves.

At twenty-seven, she'd been close to marrying a man
named Jim Hollinger. There was no possible way Jake
could have known that, no possible reason for him to
show up at such a critical time. She'd had to give back
Jim's ring, and Lord, she'd been ashamed. Jim was a
true-blue nice man. Jake was an impulsive, wandering
rogue, and he was never going to change. He'd stayed
four months. At the end of that time, he was still wearing
ragged jeans and didn't have any idea where he was
headed. She'd told him *never* to come back. And meant
it. Lord, she'd meant it. Every single time he'd shown
up in her life, she'd fallen—hook, line, sinker, soul,
fingernails, toes. And every time he left, there was a
terrible yawning gap, a wrenching loneliness, an ache in
her heart that would never ease.

She tucked the blouse into a heather pin-striped straight
skirt. Its matching jacket followed, a designer label, se-
verely tailored. Spectator pumps, a slim bracelet-style

gold watch... the austere image was not a disguise, but Anne. Polish and perfection and a control she valued. She went out regularly on Saturday nights, with men who wanted and respected the kind of woman who looked good and talked well and could hold up her head in any social gathering. Jake couldn't care less about all of that. Because her childhood had been chaos, Anne had patterned her adult life on very different lines. Jake had always been the only zigzag in the pattern...

There was no sound from the doorway. She didn't know why she suddenly glanced up... to find him there, all scraggly brows and leonine mane, the bold line of his shoulders clearly defined under the sheet he had carelessly draped around himself. Sleepy eyes were busy surveying Anne, from her figure-eight coil to her spectator pumps.

"Your slip is showing," he remarked idly.

She was too smart to jump. "Since I know you will anyway, make yourself a cup of coffee. I have to go to work." He said nothing. Wariness prickled her nerve endings as she bent to add lipstick and a handkerchief to her purse. The feeling of vulnerability was suddenly there again, unwanted and upsetting.

"The image just doesn't always work the way I think you want it to, princess," he murmured thoughtfully. "You're a striking woman, no matter how you dress. Sometimes I like the formal Anne best, actually. All marble surface, all softness underneath. A contrast that very honestly reflects the lady... Anne?"

She was picking up her briefcase from beside her small desk. "Hmm?" His comment confused her. He'd always mocked her clothing styles, always teased her about them.

"I really have come back to marry you."

Her heart stopped. She took a silent breath. "Last night I had a few glasses of champagne. This morning I won't be so easily rattled, Jake. You can take your insanity— and your suitcase—over to your grandfather's, after you've had your coffee."

"Very assertive," Jake admired gravely.

In spite of herself, Anne's lips curled in a smile. "Thank you so much."

"I haven't decided whether to try for a long, drawn-out battle or to play low-down and dirty. Do you have a preference?"

"Only for you to move away from the door."

"Low-down and dirty then," Jake decided absently.

"But it takes two to play, and one of us isn't playing." She brushed past him, her eyes averted from the mat of masculine hair on his chest. The smell of his sleep-warm flesh assaulted her nostrils. She headed rapidly for the door.

"Anne?"

"No," she called back to him. That seemed to cover everything.

"I love you to distraction."

In less than a minute, she'd snatched up her coat and let herself out the front door. Crisp September air greeted her, a dew-drenched lawn, and the special silence of the morning. She was far too early for work, but she could always pick up a cup of coffee and a newspaper somewhere . . . Her heels click-clicked on the pavement as she strode toward her MG, shivering just a little from the morning chill. She slid into the driver's seat, stuck the key into the ignition, and started the engine. For just an instant, she caught her reflection in the tiny rearview mirror. A suspicious brightness glittered in her eyes. And her fingers were trembling annoyingly on the wheel.

She and Jake were chalk and cheese. She valued stability; he was a hopeless rover. He was lazy-sleep-in to her rise-and-shine, jeans to her business suits, lackadaisical chaos to her well-ordered world. She knew exactly what she required in order to survive; she had learned the lessons when she was very young, and the lessons had been very hard and very painful.

It was not amusing to have fallen in love with the wrong man.

Slipping the car into reverse, she backed out of the

drive. You're thirty-one, Anne reminded herself. Mature enough to know certain relationships can go only so far. *Plenty* mature enough to say no to a dead-end physical relationship that has already brought more than enough heartache.

Again her eyes met their reflection in the mirror; this time there was a trace of humor in their haunted green depths. Mature? Jake could bring out the terrible two's in a hundred-year-old saint. Anne had lost control the moment she'd seen him at the party. Mature?

She loved that man. And she heartily wished that he'd never come back.

chapter 3

AT MIDMORNING, ANNE stepped out of her office with a sheaf of papers in her hand. The trust department of Yale Bank and Trust was carpeted in teal blue and paneled in dark walnut; the mood of the place, particularly on the second floor, was efficient, quiet, and formal. It suited Anne. Yale was an old-time, small, well-established bank, not in competition with the major conglomerate banks of the metropolitan area. Its specialty was trusts and estate planning; its assets were varied and closely guarded; and its stock was so zealously held that shares were rarely for sale. Conservative was the name of the game.

Anne had a nice block of that stock, and in the six years she'd been with the bank had acquired more. Trust officers were typically over fifty and balding, a stereotype that was important, actually. Authority and experience were critical to gaining the customers' trust. Fred Laird would never have given her the title two years ago, no matter how much he respected Anne, if she hadn't demonstrated her ability to bring in the high-powered accounts that the bank specialized in. Gil Rivard had been her first estate. Jake's grandfather. Anne had wanted to do that work for him, but had been uncomfortable when he later sent his friends to her. She had too much pride to want anyone's help, and she wished to owe no one favors.

She no longer needed favors from anyone. Anne was conservative, inventive, knowledgeable, and could find loopholes no one else had ever heard of in the tax laws. One customer had told her jokingly that she was more concerned with his security than he was. True.

Between her peaceful bailiwick and the noise of the new computer at the opposite end of the second floor, there was a central room where three typists worked, flanked on three sides by filing cabinets. In principle, the computer was supposed to reduce the number of files required, but banks, Mr. Laird had once told her wryly, have an intrinsic need to justify any transaction they make ten times over. Throwing away anything was anathema, a no-no. The computer regularly spit out reports someone was dying to file, even if they were never read again.

A gross exaggeration, Anne admitted dryly, but judging from the pile of paperwork on Marlene's desk, not far enough from the truth.

"You need something, Miss Blake?"

"Just a report copied." Anne waved the brunette back to her chair. "I'll do it myself; I can see you're swamped."

"Typical Monday," Marlene admitted.

A half-hour later, Anne returned from the first floor's photocopying room, juggling the folders and two cups of coffee, one of which she left on Marlene's desk. The girl looked up with a surprised thank you, but Anne was already passing.

It was not, for Anne, a typical Monday, but she was trying to get through it. At work she invariably projected a smooth, quiet-voiced serenity; she never flaunted her authority, but it was there. She'd earned it. No one could conceivably tell by looking at her that her calculator had come up with whimsical figures all morning, that she'd lost three files, that she'd shuffled the papers in her IN

basket twice and still didn't know what was in there. She
had snagged her pantyhose. Being Anne, she had a re-
placement pair in her desk drawer, but she spilled coffee
on them on her way back from the photocopying
room... The day was just not going well.

Distractedly, she pushed open the door to her office.
Her eyes were instantly drawn to the silver-wrapped
package with its gay streamers of pink ribbons. Frown-
ing, she set down the files and her coffee and closed the
office door. An unsteady pulse throbbed in her throat as
she slowly started to undo the bright wrappings.

Memories of other surprise gifts through the years
raised the color in her cheeks. The presents never arrived
on her birthday, never at Christmas. Never when she was
expecting them. *Never* anything that was suitable to be
opened in one's office, even if one locked the door and
pulled the shades over all the windows...

One peek inside the box and the pulse in her throat
went into double time. She glanced up nervously to make
sure the door was closed before carefully unfolding the
treasure. The camisole was designed like a Victorian
corset, the old-fashioned kind that cinched up the figure.

Except that there was no whalebone to viciously sever
breath. Just satin, a luscious oyster-colored satin, and a
low bodice tucked and gathered to deliberately display
the wearer's breasts so brazenly that she would certainly
catch a cold.

Unconsciously, she stroked the soft folds, her palms
stroking the luxurious satin, the fabric whispering a subtle, erotic call to her senses. Her rational mind, of course,
was already crisply cataloging objections. The gift was
terribly inappropriate. Anne's choice of lingerie was not
unfeminine, but always simple and practical. Lace and
satin—she just wasn't the type. Jake *knew* that. And
yes, it was from Jake. She didn't even need to look at
the card.

No one else would have given her a gift that was so
blatantly a sexual invitation. No one else *persisted* in

inviting her to be the kind of woman she simply wasn't. Very rapidly, she folded the camisole back into the box, feeling oddly breathless. When the lid was back on, she caught her breath again. If anyone had seen him bringing that in . . .

She buried the wrappings in her wastebasket, praying no one would knock on her door until she was done, and then hastily picked up the envelope. The note had been boldly scrawled in black ink. "Since I must have missed you, love, I went to see your Mr. Laird. All I wanted to know was if you were free for lunch. He said you were free to come to Idaho with me for two weeks."

She had to read it twice, because the first time she had obviously misunderstood. Jake would never have gone to see Laird, not even as a joke. Jake was unscrupulous and arrogant and, God knew, impulsive, but their affair had always been strictly private; he had always shown a respect for her that Anne had never questioned. She read the note a third time, sank back in her desk chair, closed her eyes, and murmured to herself, "I am a mature, rational, practical woman in full control of my life." One could not feel stalked unless one allowed oneself to become prey. She was not prey. For anyone. There was no logical reason she should feel a shudder of primitive fear dance up her vertebrae.

The thing to do was . . . open her eyes. Get up, for heaven's sake, and hide the camisole in the bottom drawer of her file cabinet, bury the note in her purse . . . Those things done, she straightened an imperceptible wrinkle in her skirt and opened the office door.

She negotiated carpet, linoleum, elevator, and more carpet all in the four and a half minutes it took to reach Mr. Laird's door, truly a record pace in her high-heeled spectators. Her tap was polite, perfectly in control.

"Come in."

She felt better the moment Mr. Laird offered her his usual distracted smile. Her boss intimidated half the people in the bank with those ice-blue eyes of his. He tolerated no inefficiency, would fire anyone he knew to be disloyal, and ruthlessly dictated policies that were not always popular. Anne had always gotten along beautifully with him. She also knew him well enough to realize that the distracted smile was a favorable augury. "Actually, I was going to call you earlier, Anne, but then I got hung up with a phone call. The White estate—I liked the way you handled all of it."

"I...thank you, Mr. Laird." Anne propped herself on the edge of the leather chair in front of his desk. Her nerves were all set to relax again when her boss handed her the White file, leaned back in his chair, and started chuckling.

Mr. Laird was *not* a chuckler. Anne's headache was instant.

The head of stiff white hair was shaking in disbelief. "But that was *not* what I was going to call you about. Gil Rivard's grandson was just in here." Another distinctly rusty chuckle escaped from his throat. "The man is crazy, absolutely crazy. I can't think of a time I have ever had such an...unusual...conversation."

Very smoothly and carefully, Anne vaulted out of the chair. "Mr. Laird..."

He waved her back down with that thoroughly uncharacteristic grin. "Here." He shifted an oblong piece of paper in her direction. "He handed me that, and asked me if I would give it to you. He's given you power of attorney and wants you to set up some sort of trust for him. Then he sat down for ten minutes, rambled on about the hummingbirds in Idaho, local politics, deep-sea fishing in Tahiti, and left." Her boss was chuckling again, though one of his eyebrows lurched up in a half-scold. "*If* you have the time? Anne, I think you could at least have mentioned to me that Gil wasn't the only iron you had in the Rivard fire."

Anne was staring at the cashier's check in her hand. Money made Mr. Laird so very happy. He loved it when his vault was chock-full. That slim little piece of paper in her hand bore a six-figure number after the dollar sign. Jake didn't have two nickels to rub together, the last she'd heard.

"And there's more that he wants to put away, Anne. For his children, he put it, even though he doesn't have any yet. He's got a wife in mind, I gather. Good Lord, though, the man doesn't even have the least idea of his own assets. He has bank accounts he hasn't checked up on in years in God knows how many states. And he may stay in Idaho for a few years, but there's no reason that state needs to benefit rather than Michigan, which is his real home base. He could be anywhere a few years from now." Mr. Laird peered at Anne through wire-rimmed lenses. "I suggested he hire an accountant to get his financial situation in order, Anne, but he didn't like that idea. He wants you and no one else. I don't know what you discussed with him, but I suppose we could stretch our policy a bit to allow you to conduct bank business out of state."

Anne's head was spinning. "It would be totally impossible for me to leave right now, anyway..."

"We could arrange something. After all, Gil Rivard has been a loyal customer of this bank for a good many years, and he's brought us a great deal of business. You've got vacation time coming..."

"Unfortunately, Mr. Laird," Anne sang out cheerfully, "there is *no possible way* I can go to Idaho at this time."

"He's kind of a modern-day adventurer, isn't he?" Her boss glanced at her, then out the window. The September sky was very blue. "His life sounds like a young man's dream. You'll probably find this ridiculous, Anne, but when I was a young man..." He focused back on her with a sudden frown. "If your backlog of work is the problem..."

"No, it's personal," Anne said. Now *there* was a word designed to catch her boss's attention. Since she'd never let on to anyone that she had a personal life, it had to come as a little shock. She took advantage of the startled look in his eyes, adding swiftly, "I didn't mean I wasn't willing to take care of Jake Rivard's finances, Mr. Laird. Only I can assure you that travel won't be necessary under any circumstances."

He took her meaning a little differently than she'd intended, but Anne left well enough alone. The talk had been interesting, she mused as she walked back to her office. She'd never had the least inkling before that Fred Laird had a secret wish to take off on a slow boat to Tahiti. His wife would be crushed. *Anne* was crushed, to see her normally pompous, conservative, and eminently logical boss get taken in by a rogue with a vagabond heart. Frankly, the whole thing was demoralizing...

So was opening up her bottom drawer after lunch to get a file on corporate bond regulations and finding a decadent satin camisole in its place. So was knowing that last night she'd come darn close to tumbling into bed with Jake Rivard about a minute and a half after he'd shown up in her life again.

Around four in the afternoon, Anne was pressing cool, smooth fingertips to her temples, having failed to take care of a single sheet of paper in her IN box. The only bright spot in the entire day had been whisking Jake's cashier's check downstairs and converting it to a nice, safe, invulnerable thirty-day CD. Not that she *wanted* to even touch his money, but at least temporarily he couldn't splurge it on silver mines or wildcat oil or swampland in Florida. It wasn't her business, of course. And it wasn't her business that the trust Jake had requested wasn't necessarily his best choice of investment tool, or that thirty days would allow someone to seriously study his best options. *Someone.* Not Anne. In the meantime, Jake was still wearing the patched jeans she remembered from high school. Over the years he'd neglected to mention that he could afford fourteen-karat-gold patches.

She rubbed her temples harder. Jake had been in town less than twenty-four hours, and already her well-ordered life was disrupted. But that was old news, really. She'd fallen just as hard, just as fast, the other times.

But not this time, Jake, she thought sadly. I tried love with you. Far too many times. More than enough to risk walking on the edge of that cliff again. It's the hot rush of a drug when you're here, but then you're gone. Sweetheart, I'm not suited to lead the life of a nomad.

Jake was waiting for her outside the bank when she left at the end of the day. Somehow, she was not surprised. An hour later, he nodded to a black-suited waiter, who then poured a sparkling Burgundy into their glasses. When the waiter was gone, Jake leaned back in his chair and regarded Anne with a faintly amused smile. "You're looking a little tired."

"I am," she admitted, glancing at the red leather wainscoting of the restaurant he'd chosen. Expensive. Terrifyingly expensive.

"Anything interesting happen at the bank today?"

She smiled sweetly. "Not really. Just a typical Monday."

With a throaty chuckle, he raised his glass. "To two weeks in the Silver Valley with you, love."

She raised her glass in return. "They'll have to ship the coffin."

"Yours or mine?"

"Mine. I'm not going to Idaho any other way, but you, Jake . . ." She took a breath, and then a sip of wine. "I will never and have never even considered trying to stop you from going anywhere you wanted to go."

Jake regarded her thoughtfully. Anne met his look for a moment and then studied the bubbling Burgundy in her glass with fascination. He'd given her fifteen minutes to change at her place before coming here, because she'd asked for that. A pale gold velvet jacket complemented the crimson dress with its pale gold hem and cowled collar; bone sandals completed the outfit. Not a hair was out of place; her perfume was fresh; she knew she looked her best.

Jake, by contrast, was wearing a red flannel shirt and navy cords. He was a disgrace, a total disgrace. And those damn sexy eyes of his wouldn't leave her alone for a minute.

She set down her wineglass and picked up a warm roll from the basket. "I returned your gift on my lunch hour," she lied, knowing full well he was waiting for her to comment on the camisole.

"Did you, now?"

"I think you had in mind a lady of a little more...formidable stature."

"Actually, I'm well aware of every dimension of the lady I bought that for."

"Is she nice?"

"When I was in high school," Jake drawled, "we used to make a little distinction between nice girls and good girls. Good girls went home and went to bed. Nice girls went to bed, and then got up and went home and went to bed." He paused. "At times she can be very nice."

Sooner or later, Anne figured, they would have to stop making inane conversation. The problem was, they always had inane conversation. Another problem was the way Jake was perfectly comfortable in a red flannel shirt when every other man in the place wore a suit. Still other problems were the way his hair had been roughly brushed back from his forehead and the bold male vibrations he sent across the table. You still want him, whispered a little voice in her head.

The waiter served a steak to Jake, which he devoured immediately, and veal parmigiano to Anne, which she pushed around the plate.

"Just try a bite," Jake coaxed. "Or if you want, we can order something else."

"No, thank you."

"Why don't you get it off your chest?"

"Why don't I get *what* off my chest?"

The waiter suddenly dipped down from behind her to

take her plate. A flush climbed up her cheeks like a glowing pink brushfire. The waiter didn't even look up. Jake chuckled.

"The worst they can do is throw us out if you start shouting," he said helpfully.

"I have never *shouted* in a public place in my life!"

"You should." Jake leaned forward, resting both elbows on the table, his silvery eyes intent on hers. "Let's hear it, Anne."

Without her dinner to push around, she had nothing to do with her hands but clutch the coffee cup. "This has nothing to do with you and me *personally*, understand? We're just talking about *you* now." Distress was mirrored in her clear green eyes as she thought about something he'd said earlier. "Jake, how *could* you have gotten involved in something as fly-by-night as *silver mines* when you... Look. How deeply are you involved? No, I really don't want to get embroiled in your personal affairs, but for godsake if you're in over your head..."

"You'd help me?"

"Don't make fun, Jake," she warned in a low voice.

His silvery eyes settled on hers. "I wasn't. And I never have. And if you've ever misunderstood that—"

She waved that aside with a motion of her fingers. Irrelevant. "The last I knew, you were tearing up your inheritance and tossing it to the four winds, but that's neither here nor there. The point is that you seem to have actually accumulated something to put away, and I really don't want to see you just gamble it away, risk it all again..."

"Exactly why I need your help," Jake agreed, claiming her frustrated little half-fist on the table. Slowly, he smoothed out her fingers, his thumb rubbing gently up and down her soft palm to her wrist. "Laird must have mentioned that I'm willing to give you full power of attorney. You can do whatever you want with everything I have. Lock all the money up in trusts so tight that I can't get my hands on it. You're going to love the Silver Valley in Idaho," he promised her.

She stiffened. "I am *not* going with you." Her hand shot away from his.

He didn't seem to notice. He was busy removing the spotless white napkin from her lap and standing up. "We might as well go if you're not even going to drink your coffee."

"I am *not* going to become involved in your personal affairs, Jake. Nor do I want your power of attorney. Ever."

"Now let's not say things we might have to take back," he said mildly. "And I do promise, Anne, that you're going with me."

Why try to talk to a red-flannel brick wall? Gritting her teeth, Anne led the way out of the restaurant and tried to force her blood pressure back down. Standing on the lamplit street, she shivered suddenly in the cold night air. A gray mist was climbing around the lampposts in whimsical little clouds. She buttoned her velvet jacket very slowly while Jake waited with an elusive half-smile.

"Ready for me to take you home and seduce you?" he asked casually.

"No."

She slipped into the car and waited for Jake to come around to his side. While the engine was warming, he leaned back for a moment and just stared at Anne. She felt his eyes sweep over her fine-boned profile, taking in the slight flush in her cheeks, the way her lashes fluttered away from him when she felt that claim of possession. She knew he'd meant what he said. A polite kiss at the door was not what he had in mind. She stared straight ahead. "I think you should see something of your grandfather. You've been in town more than a day already, and Gil—"

Jake chuckled and backed out of the parking space. "The lady will just build up anxiety by waiting, but we'll let her have her way," he told the sky. "I called Gramps earlier this afternoon to let him know we'd be there," he told Anne.

She leaned back in the seat and ignored him. Did she

have a choice? They drove in silence for a few minutes, Jake's car lapping up the freeway. "Anne?" he said finally. "The financial bit was a smoke screen. I think you know that."

"Pardon?"

"A smoke screen. An excuse." Jake flicked a glance at the rearview mirror, changed lanes, and pulled over to the shoulder of the expressway—to Anne's total horror. Cars whizzed past, headlights blinding them. She glanced out the rear window in search of approaching police cars, but Jake firmly turned her head until she was eye to eye with him. The smooth laziness was gone from his tone; his tenor was rough and sharp. "I've never wanted anyone intruding in my personal affairs, financial or otherwise, except you, Anne, but that isn't the point. Giving you an excuse to come with me was the point. If you need it, take it," he said harshly when she parted her lips to protest. "I'll invent just as many excuses as you need. All I want is two weeks with you, Anne. Two weeks to convince you to marry me. And I'm going to have those two weeks." He paused. "We're not a matched set; if you think I don't know it, you're crazy. Unfortunately, though, I just can't go on anymore without you, Anne. I've tried working myself half to death and not sleeping, and I've tried other women, but nothing works, and I'm damned tired of trying to make it without you. That's the bottom line. And you've got the same problem, now, haven't you?"

Anne just looked at him. Light and then shadow from the passing cars intermittently flashed across his face. Something tight and hard seemed to have settled in her throat. Jake had never talked that way; he'd always been an easy, slow, sensual lover, impulsive in a way she found irresistible.

Marry him? It was finally sinking in that he actually meant it. Oddly, the thought hurt her, deep inside. She'd fallen in love with the wolf who nipped at her hooks and eyes in the middle of a formal party, with the devil who dared to send an outrageous camisole to her at her sedate office. At thirty-one, though, she couldn't keep on playing. She needed roots, and Jake couldn't even define the word. Romance was a parachute jump where all the thrill was in midair, but Anne knew she couldn't live her life without something to hold on to. She'd spent a whole childhood falling.

"Jake, it's no good," she said desperately.

"We're going to have to try." Jake touched her cheek gently, then settled back and turned his attention to the road again, easing the car back onto the expressway.

"All this time, you never said anything—"

"All this time," he echoed, "I gave you every chance to find someone who would fit that mold you have in mind for a husband, Anne. Security, white picket fence, gray flannel suit—the whole bit. You've failed, honey. And I'm all through gnashing my teeth and worrying about who the hell you might be letting your hair down for, that he'd be the total ass I think you have in mind."

"I'm certainly glad you appreciate my taste in men," Anne remarked.

Jake shot her an amused glance. "Honey, a man who makes love to his wife two-point-three times a week couldn't keep you happy by a long shot. It isn't my fault you've built up these terrible misconceptions of what's important in your life. You forget I've been there when the lights were off."

Far too often, Anne thought darkly.

Jake pulled into the long, shadowed drive of his grandfather's house. A three-story stone mansion sat at the end of the drive. Warm lamps lit an impeccably landscaped lawn. Jake stopped the car, switched off the ignition, and turned to Anne, who was ostentatiously studying the scene outside. "If I didn't think you were desperately in need of a little sustenance, Anne, I'd be awfully inclined to offer you a little tangible proof..."

She got out of the car, slammed the door, and stalked deliberately toward the house.

chapter 4

GIL RIVARD WAS a perfect gentleman, certainly nothing
like his grandson. He offered Anne a brisk, affectionate
hug and a hand to hold on to as he led her through the
hall to the living room. Unconsciously, she found herself
smiling, looking with affection at the white-haired man
with the gentle gray eyes who always made it so very
clear he was glad to see her. "So our wanderer's turned
up again like the proverbial bad penny, Anne. What kind
of trouble has he been in this time?"

"Don't feed her lines, Gramps. She's sassy enough.
You two want brandy?"

"Please," Anne murmured. Her need for Dutch courage must have shown in her voice, because Jake chuckled
as he left the room. She and Gil exchanged glances.

"Your grandson..." she began gravely, and watched
Gil's fine network of crow's-feet crinkle up when he
laughed.

"I'm not responsible for his behavior, Anne," Gil told
her.

"*Someone* failed to take him into the woodshed when
he was still a child."

Gil shook his head. "You can't claim he's spoiled.

Jake's never asked for or expected anything from anyone
in his life."

"So every once in a while he has a good point or two."
She settled back in the wicker peacock chair that was
her favorite spot in the room. Jake returned with a tray
of drinks and snacks, and she listened absently to the
conversation between the two men.

The house was too monstrous for Gil to rattle around
alone in; she often worried about him. This room,
though, was where he seemed to do his real living.
Once an octagonal porch, it had been closed in with
jalousie windows; white wicker furniture and emerald-
green curtains added touches of brightness. In summer,
both sun and breezes wafted through the room; in winter, a small wood stove lent a wonderful coziness. Anne
had spent hours there over the years, and her visits had
had nothing to do with Jake. Gil had attended her high
school graduation, sitting with her grandmother; Gil
was the one she had talked to about her career goals
when she was in college; Gil had invested faith and
trust in her when she started her job at the bank. If
anyone knew of her relationship with Jake, it was Gil,
but no words had ever been spoken by either of them
on the subject. Jake's grandfather, in spite of the age
difference, had always been a special friend to Anne,
and now, she gradually relaxed in the familiar room.
At least until she realized that she seemed to be devouring the plate of cheese and fruit Jake had placed
next to her. And the cup of tea. No brandy, after all.

His eyes met hers in the distance. *The last thing you
need is alcohol when you didn't have a thing to eat at
dinner,* he telegraphed.

She smiled faintly, uncrossed her legs, strode over to
the coffee table between the two men, poured herself a
liberal glass of brandy, then returned to the curved wicker
throne chair.

Seven steps seemed to be the safest distance. If she
moved any closer to Jake, something went haywire in
her nervous system, something disgracefully sexual that

didn't belong anywhere near his grandfather and emerald cushions and the lazy conversation about Gil's antique sword collection. In his red flannel shirt and jeans, Jake looked distinctly feral. Undoubtedly a stranger would only have seen a normal-looking man with strong features and lazy humor in his silver-gray eyes, but Anne knew feral when she felt it. The man was about as trustworthy as a hungry lion let loose in a meat market; he was as unpredictable as a kite in a windstorm; he would *never* outgrow the need to take the road less traveled by...

Go with him, Anne, her heart whispered.

She quickly censored the vagrant thought, picked up the last cracker with cheese, and delicately nibbled. She was not pleased with Jake at the moment. Silver mining, the fool. So he'd finally accumulated a little money. And he would probably throw it away. Again.

Marriage to a man like Jake would mean steak one year and canned beans the next. Bleakly, Anne acknowledged to herself that beans weren't the point; it was the up-and-down lifestyle that threw her. The thought of children being tossed from one place to the next; a house all decorated just in time to move again... She'd lived that kind of life as a child with her mother. She hadn't stopped having nightmares until she was old enough to dictate her own lifestyle. Jake's life was very, very exciting; Anne's was boring. She *loved* boredom, and she apologized to no one for valuing roots and stability and lifelong friendships.

Jake's eyes met hers again, and Anne rapidly took another sip of brandy. *Look, Buster. If I want a glass of brandy, I will certainly have one.*

Your choice, Jake's eyes warned her wickedly. *I hate to have to tell you this, honey, but you're not much of a drinker. And you do tend to become endearingly amorous when you drink on an empty stomach.*

Her eyes darted to the windows, and she became intrigued by the ivy clinging to the window frames. Thoroughly irritated, she acknowledged that Jake knew too damn much about her. If she were meeting him now for the first time, she would certainly be smart enough to avoid him like the plague. The whole problem was that they'd known each other far, far too long.

Go with him, Anne, her heart whispered once more. Marriage—you know better. But what if... what if this was her last chance to be with him? What if he really never did show up in her life again, if he never made love with her again? Always, it was Jake who stood between her and the imaginary mate in the gray flannel suit he made fun of so regularly. Something always seemed to go flat when she found herself close to a commitment to someone else, a hint of panic that made no sense when Anne was totally honest with herself about exactly what she needed and wanted in a relationship.

Setting down her brandy glass, she rose restlessly from the chair and wandered to the window, staring at the fluttering leaves of the tall old maple in the yard. The night was lonely, a black sky offering no stars, a silent, cold, colorless world. She shivered, and just that suddenly felt two warm arms wrap around her from behind. Ever so naturally, Jake tugged her against the secure strength of his chest. It must have been those two sips of brandy that made her snuggle back against him like a kitten. "I love Anne," Jake remarked offhandedly to his grandfather.

She stiffened like a cat, and turned around.

Slowly, Gil stood up from the couch, an affectionate smile wreathing his features. "Then perhaps you won't be such a fool as to take off without her this time," he scolded his grandson, and added absently, "I always hoped that the two of you ..."

Anne didn't say much until the Morgan was zooming along the deserted country road. "You gave him every reason to expect great-grandchildren, she accused Jake furiously. "I just don't believe that you would involve him—"

"All I did was tell him I loved you."

Jake's voice was quiet and reasonable. From Anne's

point of view, fuel for a fire. A wisp of hair had escaped from her figure-eight bun. She blew it back. "You all but announced you were sleeping at my place!"

"Which I am."

"Which you are *not*." She stared straight ahead, at black branches dipping so low they nearly touched the roof of the car. Of all the strange roads for Jake to have taken! "You're going to drive me home, and then you're going back to spend a respectable night at your grandfather's. I don't know where you got this wild idea about marriage, but it's going no further, Jake. *Nothing* is going any further."

"You are absolutely right." He eased on the brakes and pulled the car onto the shoulder of the road. Puzzled, she stared at his jagged profile in the darkness, a profile set in stone except for the silver eyes. "Get off the throne, princess. The imperial approach sure as hell isn't going to work with me."

"I beg your—"

"Out." He slammed the door on his side as he got out of the car. Wisely, Anne ordered her heart to simmer down and her body to stay put. Jake was angry. That certainly didn't happen very often, and rarely with her, but every instinct informed her that she was safer exactly where she was. Her eyes followed Jake as he stalked around the front of the car. It was jet-black midnight outside, yet there was a liquid silver in his eyes that she could follow, and his lithe, smooth movements were those of an animal seeking prey. She would not be his prey.

Belligerently, she glared at him when he pulled her door open. "If you think I have any intention of talking to you when you're not in a reasonable mood—"

"I'm inclined to shake you silly, but I intend to do that—or see anyone else lay a little finger on you—when hell freezes over. Now get out of the car."

Well. As it happened, her legs were a little cramped. That was the problem with sports cars. Her sleek, elegant calves emerged, followed by the crimson dress from Saks and the pale gold jacket, and last the regally coiled champagne hair. Her eyes were pure emerald. "You think you're very good at intimidation—"

"And you damn well have to be retaught honesty every time we're together." She had her chin stiffly in the air about the same time her toes were. Jake must have suddenly decided she wanted to sit on the hood of his Morgan. Anne was not going to be reduced to making a fuss. If he wanted to argue in the middle of absolutely nowhere, sitting on the hood of a car, on a tree-lined lane in a thick mist . . . She shivered when his arms suddenly closed on both sides of her hips, deliberately forcing her to face him. "Honesty, Anne? You remember it?" he snapped. "You're not angry; you're scared. You think I don't know you? I know you shave your legs on Sundays and you turn into a moody little minx right before a storm. I know *you,* Anne, just as I knew you three years ago, and three years before that, and another three years earlier, too, and back when you were a prim little virgin—"

"Jake." He had never, that she could remember, hit below the belt. A flush climbed her cheeks. Jake's thumb curled under her chin, forcing her head up.

"Don't you *Jake* me. You're not shook up because I told Gramps I loved you but because you know that this round is for keeps. So put an end to it, Anne, if that's what you really want to do. Say 'Good-bye, Jake,' as if you mean it."

A most unreasonable thing to ask. Her heart was beating out triple time in dismay. Unwillingly, her eyes lifted to his, as vulnerable as a green leaf in the wind. "You want honesty, Jake?" she asked in a low voice. "We have *sex* between us. That isn't love. You want more honesty? You never talked me into doing anything I didn't want to do. I wanted you; I want you now; I will always want you . . . the whole conjugation of the verb. Anything else between us . . . would never work."

She hated Jake, had always hated Jake for making her

say things she never wanted to say. His arms suddenly wrapped her up, hugging her close, as he would a child. "That's what you think? That the only thing we ever had was sex?" She heard the note of shock in his voice. Or was it hurt? Whatever the emotion, it disappeared almost instantly. "You're joking, honey. When you were eighteen, you weren't much more than a beanpole with huge green eyes, an orphan who'd been kicked around the block just a few too many times. I suppose you think I found you beautiful even then?"

"Yes." In spite of herself, a small smile curled on her lips.

"You actually think I *wanted* you?"

"You couldn't keep your hands off me," she whispered.

"True." He hesitated, his smile dying. "But dammit, Anne, you really don't believe that sex was my only motivation..."

Her eyes half closed in sudden total weariness, her cheek snuggled against the soft red flannel of his shirt. He could tease all he wanted too; she knew the truth. So did he. And part of that truth was that just being held by him, as he was holding her now, evoked the most special kind of peace. "We make good lovers," she murmured tentatively. "We would make a terribly unhappy married pair. I don't know why you can't leave the subject alone. Don't you think we make good lovers?" Her fears and frustrations faded as she sank into the warmth and security his arms offered. A spark of Anne's coaxing humor shone in her eyes, a desire to tease Jake away from his line of questioning. She didn't want to hurt him.

Jake seemed willing to take her up on the change of subject; a devilish gleam was in his eyes. "We make very good lovers," he growled softly, his large hands framing her face. "Which is one very small reason why I want an arrangement for life."

"I'd rather take cyanide now. It would be much less painful in the long run."

A chuckle rumbled in his throat. "You're so convinced we have a problem with different lifestyles?"

"I know we do."

"That we don't share a single value that matters?"

"We don't."

"But how else are we going to get children for you, Anne? Who else would take you on but me?"

"Do you want a list of the offers I've had?" she demanded. But she was suddenly not feeling quite so lighthearted. Her perch on the car turned precarious when Jake leaned forward and buried his lips in her neck. The tickle of his breath made her shiver restlessly, like the leaves trembling in the night's whispering wind. She tried to restrain his arms, but didn't have any effect.

"So you've had offers," he murmured. "But you've failed to make a commitment to a man in a gray flannel suit, Anne. You've run out of time. And I'm tired of talking."

Obviously. Now he was into necking on deserted roads like two teenagers with no place to go. He slid his hands inside her jacket and around to the supple slope of her spine. Her troubled jade eyes met his silver ones as his came closer, suddenly holding no more humor than her own. "Jake, I'm not going to marry you," she whispered desperately.

"We're not going to talk any more about marriage," he agreed. "Just violets, Anne. You smell exactly like violets . . ."

Anne was unwilling to discuss violets. She was unwilling to sit there on top of a car in the middle of nowhere on a night turned cold. His lips coaxed, trailing sweet, persuasive kisses along the line of her stubborn jaw, up to the furrowed frown on her forehead, down over her unhappy eyes. His mouth settled finally on the most difficult obstacle, her two lips pressed firmly together, at the same time that his hands were staging a subtle guerrilla war on her back.

Suddenly, she was sliding off the hood of the car. Her

toes touched the gravel roadside; Jake cradled her legs between his. The assault of length to length was not one her heart had been expecting. Their shapes fit together with exquisite puzzlelike perfection. She needed air suddenly, a chance to regroup her scattered objections. "Jake . . ."

His mouth, hovering, sank down on her parted lips and wouldn't let go. His tongue whispered over the back of her teeth, stole deeper into her warmth, a lonely tongue seeking company. His hand went to work, rearranging the crushed folds of his corduroy jacket and her velvet one; then he molded her soft, swelling breasts into the muscles of his chest.

He was so warm, so impossibly warm. When he raised his head, his eyes met hers, pure pewter. "All I had to do was see you again," he murmured gruffly. "That was all, Anne; I didn't even have to touch you. You, looking so proper at Link's party, the respect you inspire in other people, your pride in the way you walk and move, all grace, all supple femininity . . ." A slash of a crooked smile touched his mouth. His hand brushed back a single lock of her ash-blond hair that had stolen loose. "Not always a lady, though."

Never a "lady" for him . . . A wanton heart gave in, returning pressure for pressure of soft kisses turned fierce and hungry. She threaded her fingers through his hair, loving the feel of the thick mat curling around her fingers, her palms urging him closer. He smelled like the woods. His breathing grew huskier as his hands roamed with growing insistence over territory they had no business touching, not here, not in the open countryside on a lush, dark velvet night.

"Come with me," he whispered. "Please come with me, Anne. Just for two short weeks."

His lips caught hers again, not giving her a chance to answer. Devil hands splayed on her hips and then cupped their slim softness, driving her pelvis into the cradle of his thighs, burying his arousal between them like some sweet private secret. A moan escaped from her soul and echoed out into the night's silence. "Come with me," he whispered, a sorcerer's call.

She buried her face in his throat, too weak to stand. "You knew all along I'd go with you," she said help-lessly. "I won't marry you, Jake. But if you want two weeks..." A thousand objections promptly raced through her head; she ignored all of them. Jake's eyes bored into hers, accurately taking in the yearning in her eyes, the soft flush of passion, the fear of the hurt that she was sure she had just left herself open to. The pads of his thumbs slowly smoothed the lines of her cheekbones; his features were stark and grave in the darkness. He waited; she didn't understand why. "You really want to stand here all night?" she whispered.

"I was trying to give you sixty seconds to take it back, Anne. Because after that..."

She shook her head. "I won't take it back."

They drove home in silence. Anne, exhausted, leaned her head back against the seat and studied Jake wearily from under her eyelashes. How did one go about working love out of one's system? Was it an answer, to live and breathe and survive together for two weeks, until Jake could finally see that they were at odds on the values that really counted? Was that what it would take? Was she going to have to go through another parting?

Halfway through the ride home, his hand captured hers. Her fingers explored the calluses on his palm, the feel of the firm brown flesh of his hand, so much stronger and larger than her own. I don't care what I have to go through, her heart whispered. I don't care that it will have to end again.

In the driveway, Jake tucked her into the warm hollow of his shoulder as he walked her to the door. She would have shivered without his warmth. The wind had picked up even more strength; leaves fluttered in the air; clouds had parted to uncover a bright, cold moon. Jake fitted her key in the lock, pushed open the door, and stood there. Surprise flickered in her eyes as he planted a very firm, very quick kiss on her lips. "You're so very sure all we have is sex, Anne," he murmured. "Obviously, I'm going to have to make it very clear that we have more than that. Much more."

He strode down the drive, leaving her gaping in the doorway, as unsettled as a kitten.

Only when his car was gone did Anne open the door and go inside, still unable to believe that he hadn't come in with her. So he was going to show her they had much more than just sex. Principles were fine, but she could not remember a time Jake had been interested in principles once he'd touched her. Principles had never been a prime concern to Anne after she'd touched him, either.

She wandered into her bedroom, hung up her jacket, neatly lined up her shoes, and unzipped the back of her dress. Then, on impulse, she checked the latch on the bedroom window. It was locked.

An hour later it was open, not only the latch but the window as well. Anne's elbows were on the sill, her chin cupped in her hands, and she was staring blindly out at the three-quarter moon. And she was freezing. The night air was brisk, and her dress was still unzipped in back. Not that she was inclined to move.

There had been a time in Jake's life when he had preferred entering through a window rather than a door. A whole summer, actually. It had started when she was eighteen, a night when she had been very much alone and terribly depressed. Her mother had died two weeks before. Anne had told herself a dozen times that she was not grieving, because there had never been much love between daughter and mother to grieve for. The reminders didn't seem to help. The feeling of loss kept overwhelming her; she hadn't been able to sleep ... and she had had no idea Jake was even in town until she heard the rattle in the second-story window of her grandmother's house.

Horrified, she'd unhooked the casement window before he killed himself. He had climbed up a shaky trellis, clinging to the stone wall of the house. Jake burst through

the window like Errol Flynn, give or take the nose, the
different hair color, the jeans, and a completely different
build. She'd switched on the light by her bed, smiling
as she hadn't smiled in weeks, trying to look perfectly
scandalized.

"What on *earth* do you think you're—"

"I heard about your mother." His sweat shirt was
neatly tucked into his jeans for some reason. She discovered why when he untucked it, and kings and queens
and pawns bounced all over the carpet. The chessboard
came from behind his back. "I figured you might enjoy
a game of chess."

"It's three o'clock in the morning!"

"So? You weren't sleeping."

She'd given up trying to reason with him when she
was three. It was very like Jake to do the unexpected.
It was very like Jake to totally ignore the white cotton
nightgown that barely covered her thighs, her mane of
hair all tangled around her face. Somehow she felt self-
conscious only about the faint violet shadows beneath
her eyes, because that was where he kept looking, studying her. She lost the game, in seven moves, and set up
the board again.

Somehow, they never played the second game. "Come
here, Anne," Jake said quietly.

The voice did not sound at all like Jake. It threw her,
the tender intimacy in his tone. She simply went to him.
He folded her up so fast in a huge, warm hug, holding
her . . . holding her. In a moment, the light was off, and
they were lying on her bed, and she didn't object. Emotions were exploding inside her, a terrible, terrible pain
that she didn't know how to let go of. He kept smoothing
back her hair, his touch so gentle. "You want to talk
about her?"

His voice was rough, oddly fierce. Jake had never
liked her mother. She didn't want to talk, anyway. It
hurt too much to talk. Jake was warm and vibrant and
strong, and all she wanted was to hold on to him. Jake
always understood. She didn't have to talk. She had the

frightening feeling that if he let her go, she would fall
down a steep cliff, that tears would start and never stop.
Unconsciously, she shifted even closer to him, her legs
pressing between his, her arms wrapping around his waist.
Jake held her still, his hand continuing to comb through
her hair. "Don't you dare hurt for her," he murmured.
"Don't you dare, Anne."

His lips moved down in the darkness, finding her
mouth. She closed her eyes, strange feelings flooding
through her, new feelings. Her whole body seemed to
be trembling, which made no sense. She'd trusted Jake
all her life as she trusted no one else, and his lips were
soothing on hers, soothing and warm . . . and unbelievably gentle. Tentatively, her hand groped for him, slowly
moving up his shoulder, then sliding up farther to the
hair at the nape of his neck. Such rich, thick hair. She
buried her fingers in it, unconsciously clenching as his
kiss deepened, as his other hand caressed down her spine
to the soft flesh exposed by her raised nightgown. Possessively, he cupped her bottom, drawing her into the
mold of his pelvis, his whole body suddenly so strangely
taut, tense. For a moment, she was not exactly sure what
the hardness against her abdomen was. Part of Jake, she
thought fleetingly. "It's all right," she whispered.

His lips settled on her throat. *"No."* Yet he was still
trailing kisses down her neck, under her chin, around to
her ear. She heard an odd grating sound in his throat,
and then he reached for her again, his arms wrapped
around her so tightly that they hurt. "You don't have to
be afraid, Anne. I'm not going to . . ."

But he was. She understood that. He was going to
make love to her. She should have known he'd come to
her. Jake had always come, every time there was trouble,
from the time she'd been a little girl. It was different
now. For the first time in weeks, she could feel her grief
ebbing and other, even stronger emotions overpowering
that feeling of loss.

They were new emotions, and she still felt shy when
he pulled off her nightgown, when she saw the silver

sheen in his eyes, the streak of pale moonlight on her body. Suddenly, there was no loss and depression, or perhaps those feelings had inexorably blended with others. Wild, primitive yearnings swept through her bloodstream, echoing in the call she whispered to him. The first time had to be with Jake. How could it have been with anyone else?

They were friends turned lovers. She knew him so well, trusted him so very much. He was slow and patient...and infuriating. So very like Jake. Having so immediately made a dozen momentous discoveries, she was hungry for more, the way only the newly hungry can be. She wanted so badly to be timeless Eve, and instead was eighteen-year-old Anne, who truthfully didn't know so very much. Her kneecap hit his kneecap. He chuckled. How *could* he? No lover in any romance she'd ever read chuckled. And then he actually made her laugh...a sound he rapidly muffled with a kiss.

Anne was so very careful to play by the rules in everything she did. Jake didn't seem to know any rules, encouraging her in everything she did, not seeming to care if she was awkward, acting as if there was nothing to be shy about when she was terribly and suddenly aware there were a thousand things to be shy about. What on *earth* did he think he was doing?

She could not seem to catch her breath. Laughter, then kisses that stole her breath. Tickling, and then a rough-smooth kneading that ignited fires. Soft, soft tongues played with each other, a play that suddenly wasn't play. Jake's palm was cupped over that feminine mound between her thighs, and she was whimpering, not laughing. When he moved over her, he'd already told her ever so gently what he was going to do, and she was impatient, even irritable...until she felt the thrust inside her body, shockingly intimate. Then something went wrong. Jake had hurt her.

"The pain is over," he promised. "No more, Anne. Trust me."

She did, but trust had nothing to do with this. Pagan

Eve was still only eighteen. She could talk to Jake. She'd always been able to talk to Jake. This wasn't going to work. Maybe there was something physically wrong with her. Could they discuss it? She was afraid he was going to tear her apart.

He listened; she would remember for the rest of her life how Jake had listened. How his face was carved in moonlight, how he never smiled. She would have died if he'd smiled. Instead, his lips moved, over her eyes, over her cheeks, settling on her mouth again. The kiss had sent her well on her way to euphoria before his lower body moved again, and by then her body somehow already knew the rhythm. She moved with him, mindlessly, and then, magically, everything was different.

Her flesh grew moist and silky; so did his. She was not lost, not anymore. She felt wild and free, and this strange, fierce sweetness kept building. She needed...something. So terribly. Jake kept whispering to her, coaxing her. And then night exploded into day like a flash fire. An ecstasy ripped through her that she could feel to her fingertips, an intense, rich pleasure that she had never expected in a thousand years.

After that, he wouldn't let her go. She was exhausted, but he insisted on taking her through that ecstasy again and again...

Anne closed the window. She undressed, brushed her hair, settled under the covers, and knew she wouldn't sleep.

chapter 5

THE NEXT MORNING, at the bank, Anne pushed the button for the elevator and glanced at her watch. Three minutes after ten. No one was going to shoot her for being late for the first time in six years, but all the same she was a bundle of nerves. Not only had she forgotten to set her alarm clock, but this was the second night in a row that she hadn't slept very well. Undoubtedly by coincidence, Jake had been in town two days.

Smoothing the jacket of her gray wool suit, she stepped out of the elevator. Marlene was waiting with the usual pile of notes to hand to her . . . and she was wearing an odd half-smile that made Anne pause. "Having a good day?" she asked curiously.

"Very good." Marlene chuckled. "I have a feeling your day is going to be just as good, Miss Blake."

Another girl from the typing pool gave Anne a strange look. Rather distractedly, Anne smiled a greeting at her, shifting her leather briefcase under her arm as she strode toward her office. She opened the door, and her jaw dropped.

Violets were *everywhere*, spilling all over her desk,

on the small table between the two visitors' chairs, on the low credenza against the wall, even on the carpet. The stems of the small purple blossoms had been wrapped in gay silver foil, and their fragile scent filled the air. She heard the faint giggling of the typists just behind her, yet the sound seemed to come from a mile away.

She dropped her briefcase on a chair, one of the few surfaces not covered with flowers. A white envelope was propped up in the center of the purple profusion on her desk. With trembling fingers she picked it up: *To Idaho, princess.*

There was a sudden hush behind her. In a daze, Anne half turned to see Mr. Laird's unusually florid face in the doorway, his eyes riveted to the incredible transformation of her office. "Anne, the entire place has been in an uproar for the past hour." His lips pursed and then softened. "They started arriving a half-hour ago. The tellers downstairs aren't even trying to add two and two. You've always been a puzzle to them, Anne, never giving a hint you had a private life, and now this . . ." Mr. Laird threw up a hand. "And for heaven's sake, you're five minutes late for a meeting in the conference room. Had you forgotten? And as for these being delivered to the office, frankly, it's not at all appropriate."

"It certainly isn't," Anne agreed readily. Mr. Laird was so right. Jake did terribly inappropriate things. Aroused women on wooded country roads, left them standing frustrated in doorways, invoked memories so that they couldn't sleep . . . and sent violets.

"Are you coming?" Mr. Laird inquired crisply.

"Yes." Of course she was coming. As soon as she blinked back the sweet, unexpected blur of moisture in her eyes.

Anne heard the persistent thumping on her front door just as she was arranging the last container of violets on her bookcase. Her nerves leaped in response, knowing it was Jake even before he crashed through the door in jeans and sweat shirt. "Hi," he said blandly. He took a small but lethal bite from her neck, touched her nose, and sauntered in tennis shoes past her to stare into the living room. "I'm disgusted. Really disgusted. I hoped there would be more. I don't know what on earth's wrong with the florists in this town that they don't stock more violets." He pivoted back to look at her, hands loosely on lanky hips. "Aren't you proud of me?"

The thank-you speech she'd rehearsed all afternoon went the way of a whirlwind. "Proud?" she asked blankly.

"A gentleman always sends candy and flowers to a lady. They're very appropriate gifts." He prodded her with a get-with-it gesture. "I nearly forgot." He dug into his pocket, and produced two chocolate bars, a little crushed. "The candy part. Want some?"

"No, thank you." She touched her fingers to her temples. "God, you're exhausting, Jake. Would you kindly go back outside the door, say hello, let me give you an appropriate thank you for the most beautiful flowers I've ever seen? Then we can go on from there like normal people."

He considered, and then shook his head. "I don't think so." Sheer mischief lit his eyes as he surveyed her gray designer suit, white blouse, black pumps, and the jet combs holding her hair in an impeccable twist. "Did you have a DAR meeting today?"

"Did you clean out a basement?"

"If you'd been doing what I have, you would undoubtedly have dressed in jeans, too," he protested, and cocked his head. "Well, actually, *you* probably wouldn't have dressed in jeans, sweetheart, but most people—"

"Are you going to stand there and insult me long enough for me to make coffee, or is this just a quick social visit?" Anne questioned politely.

"I wasn't insulting you. I'll bet lots of people clean their ovens dressed to go to a church bazaar."

"You'd go to the President's inauguration in a frayed shirt." Trying not to laugh, she moved swiftly into the kitchen and started to pick up the coffee pot, but he followed and stopped her by capturing her wrist in his hand.

"I want you to go outside with me for a minute or two. I'm not ashamed to be seen publicly with you, even dressed as you are," he added virtuously.

"Thank you so much."

"Are you going to be angry if I tell you I called Laird to make sure we could leave by Friday?"

"Yes."

"And I called your grandmother," Jake added as he closed the door behind them and nudged Anne toward the parking lot in back of the building. "I called Jennie partly because I've always loved her, and partly because I decided that it was the chivalrous thing to do." At Anne's horrified expression, Jake grinned. "Chivalrous. You know, like candy and flowers and no sex. Now, Anne, don't look like that. I didn't say one word to Jennie about marriage, because we're not talking about marriage anymore. I just told her that we're going to Idaho, that my intentions were more or less honorable, that I would take good care of you, and that Gramps would be delighted to hear the sound of her voice should she need anything at all over the next couple of weeks.

"Jake!" Her grandmother had always taken to Jake...reservedly where Anne was concerned, however. Anne had the sinking feeling of being pulled down into quicksand. She was all too aware that Jake must have given her grandmother the same kind of expectations he'd given Gil. Great-grandchildren-type expectations. It wasn't funny. Neither was the motor home standing at one end of the parking lot. All white, waxed, and polished.

"Uh-oh." At Anne's level stare, Jake managed to fake a look of dismay. "You were planning on a quick jet trip with return passage all paid for, weren't you? That certainly would have facilitated an easier, more rapid escape whenever you wanted to call off the adventure and run home." He shrugged. "Anne, I'm *trying* to play by your rules." He started ticking off his actions on his fingers. "I left you at the door last night, all chaste and safe. I sent you flowers and brought candy to you. I got your grandmother's permission to court you, just as if we were living in the eighteenth century. Now, I can't think of *everything*."

It was one of those times when Anne had a rough time working up any sympathy for him. She reached for the door of the motor home, then stepped up inside the door, turning back for only a moment. *"Try* to behave yourself for a full five minutes now, will you, Jake? Give it everything you've got."

The cerulean carpet was as thick and springy as a sponge beneath her feet. Rapidly, Anne's eyes trailed the length of the motor home, from the plush captain's chair and overhead berth in front, to a blue velour couch and matching chair, to a tiny but remarkably complete kitchen, fitted with everything from a microwave oven to a pull-out pantry. Thoughtfully, she stepped farther in, absently opening the refrigerator to find eleven cans of beer and three apples. Cupboards revealed three varieties of canned spaghetti, canned stew, and vitamins. She threw Jake a telling glance.

"We can't all thrive on yogurt," he said mildly. "Just look at the rest."

She did. He must be keeping the tux he'd worn to Link Cord's party at his grandfather's, because it wasn't here. The closet was empty; the drawers of the bureau were stuffed with jeans and sweaters. A double bed in back had a double sleeping bag on it. A door opened to a corner bathroom, tiny and spotless. Another door opened to what must have been intended as a shower cubicle, but instead, it housed charts and maps with pins stuck into them, a pull-out desk, and an assortment of strange tools. Picks? Chisels? She didn't ask for the details.

Her mind had shifted to racing gear the moment she'd stepped into the motor home. Jake, by contrast, had suddenly turned quiet, watching her. When she finished

exploring, she wandered back to the front, having to
maneuver around Jake's tall figure . . . and assisted totally
unnecessarily by his hands around her hips. It was a
small, natural intimacy, not contrived, just . . . Jake. Yet
it disturbed her. As if she weren't already disturbed
enough.

He popped the lid on a can of beer, which he raised
in her direction. She shook her head. "Bertha's not a
toy, Anne." A motor home named Bertha? Anne thought.
"Coeur d'Alene's loaded with all the comforts of home,
but I have to have a more accessible place to stay when
I'm working out of the mining district." Eyes locked on
her face, he sat back on the couch with one leg loosely
crossed over the other. "Idaho isn't exactly loaded with
Holiday Inns. Not in the Silver Valley."

Facing away from him, Anne explored the rest of the
cupboards. She found a lone tea bag, tentatively tested
the faucets for water, and had a Styrofoam cup in the
microwave oven seconds later.

"There are enough beds for everyone to sleep lonely,"
he said dryly. "The berth is just as comfortable as the
double bed. I meant what I said, Anne. The sleeping
arrangements are up to you."

Anne said nothing. After a minute, the signal on the
microwave pinged, and she was suddenly very busy,
searching for a spoon, stirring her tea, finding a place
to toss the tea bag . . .

"I can't read your mind, dammit. *Sit down.*"

He'd given up the lazy drinking of his beer and was
hunched forward on the couch, clearly unsettled all of a
sudden. Anne calmly took her tea to the blue velour chair,
sat down, crossed her legs, and faced Jake calmly, certain
that he couldn't see the panic inside her head. And she
was panicking.

"Do you really have that many objections to our traveling this way? It's only for a few days, Anne, three at
the most, two with the best of weather. At the end of
the two weeks, I'll send you home on a luxury jet, if

you still want to come back to Michigan."

"The motor home's fine, Jake," she said quietly.

It wasn't fine. Nothing was fine. The motor home—Bertha—was just a detail, bringing an awareness that they were going to be on top of each other. There would be no privacy, no easy escape—things she'd counted on when she'd agreed to go with him.

She sipped her tea. Truthfully, his whole campaign lacked subtlety. Skip the motor home. He'd encouraged both Jennie and Gil to anticipate cooing over great-grandchildren. He'd started a no-touch policy so they could get to know each other in a nonsexual way. In principle, she approved of the no-touch policy. In reality, her body very definitely expected attention when Jake was around; her body wasn't getting it. Her hormones were already furious, a totally unnerving situation.

And, of course, there was Jake's money. The money she never knew he had. Well, Jake could take his assets and chew them up in little pieces. That was his business, and Mr. Laird would just have to get an ulcer at the sight of the Rivard multiple assets going down the drain as far as the Yale Bank and Trust went. Except that one look at that cashier's check and her eyes had lit up at the thought of all the potential long-term gains for Jake, a nest egg she might be able to force on him before he had the chance to blow it on silver mines and heaven knew what else.

And last, the violets.

Anne dismissed the violets. They were very definitely part of the campaign, but no woman with breath in her body could have resisted the violets. It was the rest. She added up his actions on the master calculator inside her head. "I'll take the upper berth," she remarked idly.

"Fine." Jake looked relieved that she was talking.

"You've been walking all over me, Jake," she announced.

A flash of surprise lit his eyes, very quickly masked by those short black lashes of his. "We've been testing the waters," he agreed, and changed the subject. "I didn't buy you the violets so you could put them on your bookcase."

She took another sip of tea, trying to force the alien feeling of panic out of her bloodstream. "No?"

"You want to know what I really had in mind?"

Anne was not without intuition. "No."

"I had this dream last night. Of you naked in a tub of hot water. Surrounded by violet petals..."

She jumped up from the chair, tugging her prim gray suit into place. "Actually, the motor home is an excellent idea, Jake. Because at the end of two weeks, you'll be happy to hire a private plane to take me home. *That's* what this trip is about. Different lifestyles. Your adventurer to my stick-in-the-mud. Which is very funny...only not exactly. You'll see, when I replace your beer with yogurt, when my neatnik habits get to you, when day after day you have to live with the differences between us...Over the long term, we *just won't work*. And love by itself isn't worth a ripe plum; I learned that early. Married people have to speak the same language, share the same values, want to live the same way..." She shook her head. "To prove that to you, and maybe even to prove it to myself one last time, I'm willing to go to Idaho with you. But I really don't think it's going to take even two weeks for us to drive each other mad."

For some unknown reason, tears were trying to well up in her eyes. Hurriedly, she turned away, and in two steps had reached the door. The handle refused to give for a minute, but she managed to open the door on the second try. She took a step down and strode off, only vaguely aware that her next-door neighbor was pulling grocery bags from the trunk of her car, which she'd parked behind the motor home.

"Anne?" Jake's voice came from behind her.

All regal pride, she turned with the utmost patience.

"I'm leaving the motor home here, so you can put your clothes and things in place."

"You can't park here. The condo rules—"

"I fixed that."

She sighed. *"Why* am I not surprised?"

Jake had his hand on the door. His silver wolverine eyes held hers, and she felt all the fascination of captured prey. "Run your tub full of very hot water, Anne," he tossed after her thoughtfully. "I want you completely naked, darling. Leave all the lights off. Just darkness, just those petals floating all around you, clinging to that ivory skin of yours..."

He slowly shook his head, obviously in reverent appreciation of his fantasy, then closed the door. Thankfully, Anne noted, with him on the inside. She suddenly found herself staring at her neighbor, who was just as intently staring back at her, wide-eyed.

"He's a total stranger," Anne said weakly. "I've never met that man before in my life."

Her neighbor nodded.

Mesmerized, Anne stared at the ocean of slow-waving corn that rippled on all sides from east to west, north to south. There was nothing else. Just the black strip of road, a blue sky that kept on coming, and the endless cornfields. It wasn't a view she'd expected when they'd started out at two that morning.

"You haven't said a word in an hour," Jake remarked to her from the driver's seat.

Absently, she fingered the lace ruffle at the throat of her pale blue blouse. "I've either fallen in love with Iowa or I'm suffering from culture shock." Glancing at Jake, she smiled ruefully. "I just keep looking out there . . . Somewhere down those side roads are the people who feed this country. Survivors. And suddenly I feel like a parasite."

"Because you work at a bank?" His brows shot up.

"Because I just *sit* at a bank, and usually think of corn as a commodity that fluctuates on the market. Of course, banking is exactly what I want to do, but I never considered how far removed my life really is from . . . I don't know . . . *real* work."

He shook his head. "You *do* real work, foolish one. You make it possible for that farmer out there to buy his farm, to keep operating through the bad years, to build up a heritage for his kids."

His instant defense of her work surprised her; she'd always thought Jake felt more amusement than respect for anyone who worked at a desk. "That was almost a nice thing to say," she ventured casually.

Jake shot her a crooked grin. "You love what you do, and you're good at it. Did you think I never noticed?"

"Good Lord, I think that was another nice thing to say."

Jake chuckled. "Maybe you could blend both worlds, and open up your bank vault in bib overalls."

Anne smoothed her mauve wool skirt and thought, We have to stop having these nice, easy conversations. She'd chattered to him all morning, laughing over absolutely nothing, forgetting completely that it wasn't just Jake next to her, but Jake-who-came-back-threatening-marriage-this-time. "Do you want a snack?" she asked suddenly.

"Restless, Anne?"

"Terribly," she lied, as she got up, ducking under the overhead berth to head to the back of the motor home. "I warned you I wasn't a very good traveler, Jake, much less a camper. I can't imagine where we're going to find a place to stay in country like this tonight."

"Fildekirky, Iowa," Jake called back to her.

In spite of herself, she chuckled at the sound of the name, and started opening cupboards.

"If you find a doughnut back there . . ."

She brought him a bag of dried pineapple slices, which would be much better for him than a doughnut and would still satisfy his sweet tooth, then returned to the miniature kitchen to make herself a cup of peppermint tea. It still amazed her that she could get up anytime she liked and make a cup of peppermint tea while driving.

A moment later, she took a sip of her brew, glancing around before going back to sit by Jake. The motor home, she decided, was a symbol of the impermanence of Jake's lifestyle. It represented the unbridgeable distance between them . . . but she seemed to be falling in love with the darned thing. Everything was so meticulously neat; there was a place for everything, home comforts begging to be taken advantage of.

She'd had three days to rearrange everything, of course. Her yogurt had joined his beer; fresh fruits and vegetables supplemented his canned goods; sleeping bags had been replaced by percale sheets on both the double bed and her berth. Next to his paper plates and plastic forks were china and sterling. Her wardrobe provided a contrast to his; traveling suits to his jeans, high-heeled shoes to his tennies.

She'd deliberately gone overboard, right down to the brands of toothpaste she'd chosen, in an effort to impress Jake that their values were terribly different even in the little things. Taking a minute to reapply lipstick in their tiny bathroom, Anne took in her reflection, from the high-throated blouse and modest violet skirt to the prim coil of hair at the nape of her neck. The image was honestly Anne, soft fabrics and gentle colors and classic styles. She was not flamboyant and never would be; she was not at all the kind of woman she expected Jake to end up with.

Fleetingly, her soft jade eyes met their reflection in the mirror; her expression was oddly distressed at that moment. Surprisingly, she was happy to be with Jake. She had always been all too happy to be with Jake, at least until he'd brought up the subject of marriage. She knew that yogurt versus beer wasn't the issue; rather, the crux of the matter was their different systems of values. Her craving for roots and stability and order . . . Lord, you're boring, she told the mirror wryly.

And the man hadn't touched her since she'd agreed to the trip. His restraint was making her nervous. She'd heard what he said about proving they had something more than sex between them, but Jake's blood had certainly never run tepid before . . . You're *supposed* to be boring him, she reminded herself. You should be happy he's keeping his hands to himself.

Still, though, a little kiss wouldn't cost him much, her libido grumbled. Would you stop *that?* Grabbing a newspaper, she walked back to the captain's chair next to Jake, wearing her most formal, boring smile. "I'm going to read aloud to you from *The Wall Street Journal* so you won't get restless," she announced to him cheerfully. "Do you want to hear about common stocks or blue chips first, Jake?"

His crooked grin had a little too much Chesire Cat in it for Anne to feel comfortable. She decided on blue chips. Most days, they even bored *her.*

The dot on the map for Fildekirky was an overstatement. Anne, buried under campground directories and road maps, was by now heartily sick of cornfields. Once she'd directed Jake to the expressway exit he wanted, her nerves quieted down with an expectation that never materialized.

"This is *it?*" she asked him unbelievingly.

A shabby little diner sat on one corner, a gas station on another. Three pickup trucks took up the restaurant's parking lot, such as it was. A mongrel dog wandered along the middle of the main street. Late afternoon sun was pouring down in long yellow rays on the silence.

"I had a feeling your love affair with Iowa wouldn't last," Jake said lazily. "Not that you can judge any state by the view from its highways. Tomorrow will be quite different, Anne, but I have a feeling the campground will surprise you. I've been here before."

The campground did surprise her. There were trees.

Gingerly, Anne stepped out of the motor home as Jake sauntered into a wooden A-frame building to check in. She felt like a toddler just learning to walk as her feet touched solid ground.

The A-frame and huge maples blocked her view of the actual campground. She'd already decided the trees were imported. Across the road were another five trillion acres of farmland and nothing else. At least there was a huge green tractor to relieve the monotony, but she had no real hope for the view behind the thick row of bushes and maple trees.

She glanced toward the door of the A-frame. Jake was taking forever. Smells assaulted her nostrils, the scents of rich brown earth and green leaves, not unpleasant. Rubbing at a kink in her neck from all the traveling, she wandered around one side of the building. A cool breeze had picked up the hint of a September night; a few of the maple leaves had started to turn gold and russet. The campground owners had planted a wild profusion of marigolds and asters, their perky colors splashing over the stone walk as she meandered farther. The place wasn't totally uncivilized...

A fat white duck suddenly waddled in her direction, squawking belligerently. Startled, Anne glanced up. Her eyes widened in surprise. A narrow creek wandered like a serpent between shaded campsites; in the middle of the creek was a strange redwood structure that looked like a miniature fort mounted on wooden stilts with a rustic ladder leading up to its entrance. The place was almost pretty; the ambience had clearly been created to provide a quiet night's rest for a stranger... barring the ducks.

White duck had friends. All of them seemed to catch sight of her at the same time, and instantly waddled forward to welcome her. There seemed to be thousands of them... Well, four dozen, anyway. Fat ducks, skinny ones, some white and some brightly feathered, all quacking unlyrically. Laughing helplessly, Anne bent down to pet one, and found a dozen yellow beaks very gently trying to devour her hand.

"It sounds good, but don't believe a word you hear," Jake suggested dryly from behind her.

"They're obviously hungry." She blinked. The squawking cacophony reached a dangerous decibel level. "Jake, they're *terribly* hungry..."

"We're just an hour ahead of the usual camper trade. By eight o'clock, those ducks will be so full they'll sink if they try to swim, and Rochester—the owner of the campground—will pocket mucho dinero for every wee handful of feed he sells."

"Oh? He sells the feed?" Anne questioned absently, her hand still stroking the silky feathers of the closest duck. She glanced up a moment later to find Jake studying her with one of his half-baked grins.

"Anne, don't you think you'd better free yourself from your admirers before they nibble your immaculate nylon stockings to shreds?"

Anne threw him a speaking glance and waded through the ruffled feathers and outraged quacks to head for the door of the A-frame office. The screen door clapped shut behind her as she entered. Inside was a dizzying array of products for sale, from milk to *Penthouse* magazine, from ivory chess sets to canned soup. Behind the long counter, she noticed travel guides, diapers next to spark plugs, sunglasses next to aspirin. A short, cigar-smoking man stood waiting; a plaid shirt was stretched tightly over his watermelon-sized stomach. "Well, hi, little honey."

"Hi." She spotted the cardboard box filled with cellophane-wrapped packages of duck feed. Fifty cents for a handful. Robbery, sheer robbery. Instinctively, Anne clutched her purse in tight fingers for a second. She never even allowed pennies to collect in the bottom of her purse; it wasn't in her nature to let herself be taken in by the owner of a tourist trap. On the other hand, it wasn't in her nature to let the poor ducks be victimized, either.

"One or two, ma'am?"

Her voice seemed to come from a distance as her left hand forced her right hand to release its hold on her purse. "I'll take all of it," she told the man grimly.

"I beg your pardon, ma'am?"

"If they eat all of what you have in that box in a day, I'll take it all," Anne enunciated clearly.

Jake burst out laughing when he saw her emerge from the building laden with little cellophane packages, but the ducks bore down on her like an attacking little army.

"Darn it! Don't you say one word," she ordered Jake.

He reached her side in seconds and dived for the two bags she dropped, at the same time shooing away the persistent white duck who wanted her skirt hem for dinner. She tossed a cascade of mixed corn and other grain to the ground. The ducks dived for it with their beaks, their fat, feathered bottoms wiggling furiously in the air. Anne heard herself helplessly giggling, but there wasn't time to enjoy the scene. Suddenly, dozens of beaks were poised expectantly in her direction again. Jake reached in front of her with another bag. She started laughing again as she tossed another handful of grain on the ground. "You don't have to tell me this is ridiculous. It just went against the grain to know the poor creatures had to wait for a bunch of tourists to dole out their dinner. It's cruel, Jake..."

"Went against the grain?" Jake groaned.

That started more giggles. The white duck sat on Anne's foot. She ripped open three bags at once, and then had to swoop down and chase one brightly feathered bird who was taking off with an empty cellophane package in its beak, like a prize. When all the bags were empty, she held up her empty hands. "That's all," she told the ducks. "You guys are supposed to be full."

Full or not, the ducks were irritated. They waddled off to splash one by one in the S-shaped creek beyond the maple trees, with a loud chorus of disgruntled quacks. "Did you hear that?" Anne brushed a strand of hair from her cheek, put her hands on her hips, and suddenly whirled to face Jake indignantly. "They're maligning my character. After going through all th-this..."

Her tongue seemed to trip. Jake was no longer smiling. He was staring at her, his silver-gray eyes intensely warm on hers. Boldly warm, vibrant. She caught her breath in sudden confusion. "I-I know it was...foolish," she said hesitantly. "I don't know what got into me; that man is a thief. Lord, I don't even know anything about animals, let alone ducks."

"Yes, you do. You had a puppy once, don't you

remember?" Jake crumpled the empty cellophane packages and tossed them into the closest litter bin, then brushed against Anne's shoulder as he led her back to the motor home. "You and that puppy were inseparable. Then, when your mother married what's-his-name, you had to give the pup away. The next time I saw you, I tried to give you a kitten. Have you forgotten that, too, Anne? But you wouldn't take it. You said you'd never again accept anything that could later be taken away from you."

"Well . . ." She remembered, unwillingly; that hadn't been the happiest time of her life. She gave a short, quick, cover-up laugh as Jake started the motor home to drive them to their campsite. "You have a good memory, Jake," she said lightly. "I couldn't have been more than seven, and you were no more than ten at the time."

"You adored that puppy. And you're right, I was exactly ten, but I can still remember wishing your mother would fall into a deep, dark pit." Jake flashed her a crooked smile so fast she thought she'd imagined the flecks of steel in his eyes, and the unexpectedly bitter comment about her mother. "You were very pretty when you were seven."

She couldn't help chuckling. "You like pigtails, do you?"

"What I like, Anne," Jake said quietly, "is your laughter."

chapter 6

DINNER WAS OVER, and Anne sighed with satisfaction as she picked up their plates from the small table. Jake had just gone outside. Something to do with starting their hot-water heater. Anne had seen the myriad dials and compartments on the side of the motor home, but she was more interested in playing housewife in the dollhouse on wheels, for the moment.

The dishes were few. Jake had grilled steaks outside, and Anne had complemented them with baked potatoes dripping with melted cheese and bacon bits, and a salad of fresh greens. She usually found cleaning up a nuisance, but it wasn't so bad with only two plates and a few pieces of silverware in the tiny powder-blue porcelain sink. After adding soap and water, she reached to pick up the two empty wineglasses, and noticed a pair of keys next to Jake's plate.

Pushing open the door, she called out, "There's already plenty of hot water. You don't have to worry."

"I wasn't sure. The pilot light's kind of fussy." He was bending over the dials, looking as blissful as a teenage boy with a hot rod.

Anne chuckled, and then remembered. "What are the keys on the table for?"

"I thought we could both use a chance to spruce up after a long day of traveling. One key's for the shower room for you. The other's for the hot tub for me," he said absently.

"Sounds good," she agreed, and went back to her chores. She swiped at the table with a damp sponge, washed the two crystal goblets in steaming water, and frowned. A moment later she pushed open the door again. *"What* hot tub?" she called out.

It had turned dark since they'd sat down to dinner. Jake emerged from behind the motor home, his wolfish features accented by the yellow light of the outdoor lamp. He wiped one hand on the hip of his jeans, motioning vaguely to her with a screwdriver in the other hand. "You'll be happier with the shower, Anne. Take my word for it."

He disappeared into the shadows; she returned inside. Two china plates, two sets of silver, two salad plates . . . She unplugged the drain and watched the water swirl in rapid circles on its way down. Weariness flooded through her. It wasn't an unpleasant sensation, just the kind of fatigue that came from traveling. Or perhaps that was how she excused a sudden unsettled feeling. The circle of light around the tiny kitchen area felt like an oasis. To her left was the double bed where Jake would sleep; to her right was the upper berth where she was sleeping—of course. Jake had made that clear. Twice. Her eyes flicked again to the keys on the kitchen table.

The motor-home door clattered open behind her; she all but jumped. "Actually, I would prefer the hot tub," she remarked promptly, as if they were in the middle of a conversation.

Jake didn't have any problem following her. "No, you wouldn't." He motioned toward the window in front of her. *"There* is the hot tub, honey." She peered out at the crazy-looking redwood structure she'd noticed before, the one that resembled a child's fort. At the moment, it was hidden in dusky shadows, but she could still make out the ladder and the redwood siding. Suddenly, as she peered at it, she realized that it had no roof.

"Bathing under the stars isn't at all your style, Anne. It's not as if you'd brought a bathing suit. In the shower, you'll have your privacy."

"Privacy? You've got a key that locks the gate, haven't you?"

He brushed past her, a hand just drifting along the small of her back as he moved by to put his tool box away. "Forget it, Anne. The women's shower is more private. The last time I was here, a family of six descended on the hot tub while I was soaking in it. They had a key, too. That didn't bother me, but it would certainly bother you."

She could still feel the imprint of his splayed palm on her back. "Only two other motor homes have come in since we've been here. They're both retired couples, and both already have their lights out, for heaven's sake." He was facing away from her, almost as if he wasn't listening, and was opening drawers to get fresh clothes. "I'll get the towels," she said swiftly.

He stood up straight, so she could get past him. All very considerate. And offering her the shower, under the circumstances, was very considerate, too. Anne valued her privacy... There was no reason at all for her to feel miffed. Jake wasn't the type to get upset if other people saw him naked; she very definitely wasn't into community baths.

Fine. Only there wasn't any "community" to worry about. Except for the "community" of the two of them. And in total darkness, with Jake, she was hardly worried about anyone else anyway. *Bathing under the stars isn't at all your style, Anne*... She piled two thick terry-cloth towels in her arms, added her soft navy velour robe, and felt as if there were five tons of irritation in her bloodstream. No one liked to be *pegged*.

When she moved past him again, Jake moved forward to get out of her way. The motor home had ample space except when two adults were trying to negotiate the walkway at the same time. It took some effort to avoid touching each other—and Jake was certainly making the effort. Anne added a hairbrush to her pile of bath supplies. "Unless you have some objection, I'd prefer the tub over the shower," she said stiffly.

"Why would I have any objection?" He paused. "What's wrong?"

"Nothing is wrong."

They both stepped outside into the darkness. A little wispy mist was starting to rise from the creek, illuminated by occasional yellow yard lights strung haphazardly through the camp's park. The charcoal dusk seemed to mute all sounds. It was nearing ten. The two other mobile homes in the distance were dark; they might as well not have existed.

Jake raised his arm and just looked at her. Anne walked into the hollow of his shoulder with a small smile and they started along the shadowed path. Jake's arm offered a simple promise of reassurance, as if her body had just plugged into a powerful source of warmth. She had a sudden whim to be kissed in Iowa.

Their eyes met, and Jake's lips suddenly curled in an almost imperceptible smile. Anne's lashes lowered at the speed of light. "You can't use the motor home for daily travel around Idaho, can you?" she said.

"I drive a jeep, which I keep there. And the motor home isn't the only place I lay my head, Anne, but I'd prefer to save a few surprises—most of the surprises—until we get there."

"You haven't really told me much about what you do in Idaho. Just knowing you're involved in silver mines doesn't tell me much."

"Anything to do with silver doesn't make any sense until you see it. As you will, Anne." He shifted the clothes under his free arm. "In the meantime, somehow I didn't expect you to spend your days staring at cornfields."

"No?" she asked wryly. "What else did you want me to look at?"

"Finances. Mine. The ones you told your boss you would handle."

His voice was light, but Anne's mood changed abruptly. "Then he'll have to fire me. Jake, that's between you and you, your money. Don't play games."

"I'm not playing games. I want a trust. You're a trust officer."

She pushed a branch out of their way as they neared the redwood structure. Was he teasing? Unfortunately, she'd always found it very difficult to view finances in a humorous light. "If I *were* to handle your business— which I will *not* do—the last thing I would set up for you is a trust. A trust is set up primarily to protect heirs, so—"

"Exactly," he said swiftly.

"Pardon?"

"Heirs, Anne. That's exactly what I've in mind. Heirs out of wedlock, since we're no longer talking marriage."

Anne's heart skipped a beat and a half. "Well, fine then," she said cheerfully. "Give me the names and Social Security numbers of your illegitimate children, Jake, and then if you absolutely insist..."

His low, throaty laughter echoed in the stillness. "At least you didn't panic when I said the word, sassy."

The word *marriage*. Anne hugged the towels and robe to her chest, suddenly unable to concentrate.

At the foot of the wooden ladder, Jake offered, "If you'd rather have the hot tub to yourself, I'll wait here until you've had a turn."

"Don't be silly," Anne said irritably. They were both adults; it was dark; and they'd certainly seen each other's bare bottoms before. Jake's arm on her shoulder could not have been more brotherly, and furthermore, she resented being treated like a prudish Victorian miss.

Her calf muscles tightened as she mounted the steps ahead of him. There were no yellow camp lights near

the tub house. She reached out in search of something
to hold on to as she climbed up to the tub; she could
barely see the ladder. The owner was rather eccentric,
Anne decided, between his ducks and a hot tub built in
the air.

"Can you see to unlock the door?" she asked once
they'd both reached the platform at the top of the ladder.

"My night vision's always been better than yours,"
Jake replied.

"Hate carrots," Anne murmured absently. He opened
the wooden gate, ushered her into the enclosure, and
relatched it with the two of them locked inside. Vaguely,
she could make out a narrow deck surrounding a square
pool large enough for perhaps six adults to sit in. Steam
rose from the surface, a stark contrast to the chilly night
air. The stars above the redwood fence seemed hung so
low as to be touchable.

Anne set down the towels, heard Jake popping the
buttons on his flannel shirt, and froze for one odd second.
From behind her, she heard shoes clump on the deck.
Then a zipper being pulled down. A zipper had such a
distinct sound . . . Instantly she decided that she would
definitely prefer to bathe alone. Jake could go first; she
could go first; it didn't make any difference. Just not
together. Only it was too late to make that decision . . .

When she no longer heard the sounds of clothing being
removed, she hurried to fill the silence. "The air is absolutely freezing," she mentioned with a little laugh.

"And the water is very, very warm. You won't be
cold, Anne."

Hmm. The water surged noisily when he stepped in;
Anne's eyes darted nervously to the wooden gate.

"It's locked," he assured her. The thread of lazy humor in his voice was unmistakable. "I could have sworn
you could hardly wait to get in the hot tub."

"I can't," she agreed vaguely, and dropped down on
the rough wooden bench by the towels. She slid off her
pumps slowly, one at a time, and set them neatly side
by side under the bench. She felt . . . set up. Stepping

back into the shadows, she turned away from Jake and reached under her skirt to pull down her pantyhose, not a graceful action at the best of times.

"Anne?"

She refused to look up. The button on her skirt wouldn't budge, probably because her fingers had suddenly turned cold and clumsy. The zipper got caught on the sole stray thread in the placket. Finally, the skirt was off and folded neatly on the bench. Her pulse pounded as if she were having an anxiety attack. She felt like a stripper about to walk on stage for the first time.

Her half-slip had turned icy the way only cold satin can. Night air whispered intimately up her legs. If the wind had been a man, she would have slapped it for its brash familiarity with that feminine triangle between her thighs. Still turned away from Jake, she started undoing the dozen tiny pearl buttons on her blue blouse.

She could feel Jake's eyes on her back, waiting. He *knew* what she was feeling. *He* was the one who'd shifted their relationship into neutral, and he knew perfectly well that it put nakedness in a different light. Undressing for a lover was one thing, but she was not supposed to want an intimate relationship with him these two weeks. She didn't. *Not again, Anne, you'll go to pieces when it's over*. So . . . it should be nothing, slipping off a few clothes in the dark. Jake *had* seen her nude before; they were both adults; and Jake had made it very clear that he wasn't going to make a pass. She had no reason at all to feel suddenly as vulnerable and fragile as a cotton puff.

Slowly, she pulled off her blouse, one sleeve and then the other. Pearl-smooth shoulders gleamed their softness from the dark water's reflection. She could keep her bra and panties on, of course; they covered more than a bathing suit. She could keep them on if she was willing to admit to herself that she still wanted him, that she cared too much, that nakedness plus closeness plus Jake was a very risky combination in her mind. Her limbs moved like satin in shadow as she unhooked the front catch of her bra. Her bare breasts protested the sudden exposure to the cold, and the nipples tightened vulnerably.

"Turn around, Anne." His voice soft, the humor all gone. Just a husky, vibrant baritone talking only to that very tiny, very primitive part of Anne...

"I'll be in in a moment." She rapidly stripped off the half-slip and panties, and her whole body began to tremble with cold. She turned toward the tub then, head lowered as she carefully negotiated the steps. The steaming hot water surged around her slim calves, then her waist, and she hurriedly crouched down so that the water came up to her shoulders.

She took a breath. "Feels good," she offered lightly, and forced her legs to stretch out under the cover of the soothing dark water.

Jake said nothing. His face was in shadow, but he was looking at her. His arms were stretched out on the sides of the tub, and gleamed golden in the darkness. His hair had picked up the silver of the stars, and was ruffled like thick, rough fur. The eyes pinned on hers were distinctly a man's, silvery, intense, opaque... She groped for an innocuous conversational gambit.

None occurred to her.

Very slowly, like a hunter being careful not to frighten a wary doe, Jake got out of the tub and reached for something to the side. She heard a click, understanding it seconds later. The concealing black waters turned iridescent turquoise, suddenly lit by three circular spotlights in the bottom of the pool. Her limbs turned to stone, locked in helpless, vulnerable display. Jake's nudity was just as clearly revealed, as he rejoined her in the tub, yet he looked neither helpless nor vulnerable.

Her breath seemed to have caught somewhere between her throat and her lungs, locked there. He was a beautiful man, just as he had been a beautiful lover. His body was sleek and strong and virile, with skin several shades darker than hers. She remembered too much, too fast. Still, she found herself staring. Droplets of water clung to his shoulders; the silver strands of his chest hair gleamed against his darker flesh in the water. It was so like Jake, the casual way he balanced himself lazily, one leg hooked over a step. He sat motionless, watching her face, not her body. And when she looked up, his dark eyes fastened on hers and refused to let go.

"That wasn't fair, was it?" he said quietly. "Turning on the lights."

"No."

His voice was low, gentle. "There were times I remembered the look of you in my dreams. They never measured up to how beautiful you really are, Anne." He added, "Do you want me to turn off the light?"

"What I really want..." There was something in her throat, some strange, hoarse catch that made the words come out like a whispered plea. "I can't seem to... move."

His hands reached out and claimed hers, drawing her through the water toward him, cradling her instantly in his warm, slippery limbs. Anne wrapped her arms around his waist as if he were a lifeline, the blood surging through her veins, her cheek nestled against his shoulder. The water lapped and soothed, lapped and soothed, its heat forcing warmth back into her chilled limbs. Jake stroked back her hair, pressing small, firm kisses on her forehead.

In the water, her own flesh looked strange to her, all white next to his, all translucent, a voluptuous image of curves and tucks that was so unlike the images she had of herself. Her lips searched for his, suddenly desperately hungry for the feeling of closeness his touch could give her, had always given her. She found what she was looking for; her mouth clung to his, drinking him in, invading his mouth with a liquid-soft tongue. Limbs tangled around limbs, drawn to each other in the dark solitude. It had been too long, her body told her, too long since he'd touched her and held her.

Jake was her haven. Her mind explained patiently that that made no sense. Her heart knew different truths. His palm glided over her breast and rib, down to her hip and thigh, and her breath caught. Slowly, he loosened her arms, his lips dipping down to the warm, damp, exposed hollow of her shoulder. "Whatever you think, I didn't intend this," he murmured. "But then, you were so foolish, sweet. You stood there worrying about every item of clothing that had to come off, almost as if you were afraid, as if you were a virgin again..."

"You know better," she whispered into his throat.

"I know better," he agreed huskily. "I know you when a dark storm is haunting your eyes and your lips are trembling and your legs are wrapped around mine..."

His mouth claimed hers, fierce, sweet, aching, hard. Almost roughly, his fingers combed through her hair. Hairpins went flying, and a cascade of ash-blond hair came tumbling down, crushed in his hands. Rapids rushed through her bloodstream, a violent, terrible shiver of vulnerability. She was suddenly floating free in the water, propelled by Jake's rough stroke away from the side. There was only Jake to hold on to in a liquid world without gravity. A low, guttural cry escaped from her throat when he raised her up from the water and touched his tongue to her breast. His tongue was moving like the lash of a whip...only tenderly. Tender, sweet lashes.

"Tell me," he whispered.

She shook her head helplessly. Tell him...what? About the hot water and the cold, cold air and the sky trying to light the entire world with stars...Tell him about the fire in her soul? Air and water and fire, an elemental cry that echoed through her bloodstream until the fierce, wild yearning was out of control...But it changed nothing. He had a power over her no other man had...but he already knew that.

"Tell me you don't remember," he went on, still whispering. "Tell me you don't feel the same anymore, that this makes no difference. Tell me what you *don't* want, Anne..." His hands roamed over her water-silkened flesh, his lips pressed into her throat. Her fingers curled in the wet fur on his chest, and she could feel his heart pounding. She could feel her own heart pounding.

So silent, the whole rest of the world. Just the rasp of his breathing and then the pressure of his mouth on hers, the smooth, warm feel of the water and the blend of limb to limb, inseparable. A sensation that she was going to fall and never stop falling... "Lord, I want you, Jake," she whispered. "Don't let go..."

She was so safe, safe and wonderfully free and alive, when he held her. Yearning ached through her in a warm, long quiver; dynamite growing desperate to explode...

The rattle of wooden gate seemed to come from a thousand miles away. Jake's fingers suddenly dug into her flesh, startling her. Even before the gate creaked open, he'd whirled her behind him and pinned her against the rough side of the tub.

"Mr. Rivard?" A pair of fox eyes peered at them in the glow of the lights beneath the water. "I was mighty worried when I noticed the yard lights were out in this part of the campground. We were having trouble with the water temperature yesterday, and I—"

"Hit the light switch," Jake said brusquely.

"Beg your pardon? I—"

"Now."

He hit the switch. The pool lights went out instantly; the water turned black. Anne buried her face in Jake's shoulderblades and closed her eyes.

"I had the thermostat repaired yesterday, but nobody's reserved the tub since then, until you did, and I thought I should check. I mean I never meant to disturb you..."

The man was embarrassed and didn't know how to make his escape. Jake handled him, in another world. The real world. Shame rippled painfully through Anne. She'd always known the relationship had no foundation to sustain it other than sex, yet so easily, so readily she'd just...

Everything was suddenly violently wrong. Her head ached; clouds had formed a cloak over the stars; and cold air dipped down inside the wooden gates and whipped at her damp hair. Her heart was still trying to beat down its disappointment at not having her sexual needs satisfied... *sexual* being the operative word, a voice in her head scolded. She was insane to have made this trip...

She heard the latch of the gate and knew the man had left. Jake loosened his fiercely protective hold, and Anne was free to breathe again. And she did breathe, her eyes averted.

"Anne . . ."

A finger cocked up her chin. She batted it away, and surged past him and out of the water, her skin tightening as the cold night air raced over her dripping limbs. She reached for a towel, then rapidly changed her mind and grabbed up her robe, which she swiftly belted around her still-soaking body.

"Take it easy, Anne," Jake said slowly, quietly coming up behind her.

"I'm not particularly proud of myself, Jake," Anne shot back, "so just lay off." Her hands were shaking as she grabbed the rest of her things and tried to tug open the gate. It wouldn't give.

"He relocked it and I have the key. Just a moment." Deftly, Jake got into his jeans and pulled a sweat shirt over his head. Anne saw the moody look in his eyes and averted her gaze. His jaw was tight, but he wasn't angry. There was just a certain stillness about him that made her want to bite the inside of her lip; she wanted out of here. Out and completely away from him.

He stuck the key in the lock, but claimed her arm before she could open the gate. "It doesn't make sense," he insisted, "to fight something we both want."

"We've *been* there," Anne hissed. "Jake, you know that. I don't know why I agreed to come. All that's going to happen is that we'll end up sleeping together again and building these . . . ties . . . and then I'll go back to being Anne and you'll go back to being Jake, and I can't *handle* that again. You'll go off to heaven knows where—"

Jake brushed a loose strand of hair from her cheek, so tenderly that she could have hit him. *"With you."*

"No! I don't *want* that kind of life; I can't *handle* it; I don't *need* it . . ." She pivoted, turned the small brass key in the door and hurried down the wooden ladder into the frigid night.

Jake didn't catch up with her until she was in the motor home, reaching in a drawer for her hair dryer. Her hair was drenched and took a long time to dry.

Jake took the dryer from her hand and dried her hair for her. Over the steady whine of the hair dryer, she gradually calmed down, not really from discipline but rather from exhaustion. If Jake had said one word . . . but he said nothing at all. Once her hair was dry, he pulled a nightgown over her head, helped her into the upper berth, and tucked her into her own pink comforter. "You're not going home," he whispered. "I know exactly what you have in mind at the end of the two weeks, Anne— leaving. All right—if that's how you feel then. But you're not going home before the two weeks are up. Hear me?"

She heard him.

chapter 7

LAZILY, ANNE'S LASHES fluttered open. A thin band of sunlight stole through the curtains surrounding her upper berth. The droning of the engine told her that the motor home was on the road. Groggily, she rolled over, tugging her comforter with her, and with a sleepy yawn parted the curtains enough to see out.

The rich, black farmland and the cornfields had disappeared, as had the gentle, long rolls of western Iowa. Pale wheat now stretched along both sides of the serpentine road, except where a gnarled gray butte jutted up from nowhere. The arid landscape was strangely colorless, stark and bleak. Fences suggested cattle land, yet she saw no sign of life. Or houses. Or even trees . . . Then suddenly a clump of cottonwoods whizzed by as Jake took a curve. The trees were beaten and bent by the kind of wind Anne could only imagine might blow through here and never stop.

She climbed down from the bunk and went to stand behind Jake. "Good Lord, where are we? How on *earth* long have you been driving?"

"Since two this morning. I had in mind your seeing

91

the Badlands by dawn, but couldn't quite make that. On the other hand, you slept in to just about the right time." His eyes flickered up to meet her gaze in the rearview mirror, and he immediately flashed her a crooked smile. "When you get around to it, I'd sell my soul for a cup of coffee."

"Would you, now?" She yawned and shook herself sleepily, still half immersed in the crazy dream she'd awakened from. She'd been standing stark-naked in a room, explaining to the silver-eyed rogue in front of her the futility of investing in high-risk, low-yield stocks, and he'd been listening, dressed in a gray flannel suit, interrupting her only to mention that he wanted to live in a two-story brick house in the country. She yawned again. The dream vaguely irritated her. She expected even her unconscious to have better sense, and Freud could take a hike.

Her bare toes sank into the lush blue carpet as Anne rapidly disappeared into the bathroom, splashed her face with cool water, and stared sleepy-eyed at the mouth that had all but begged Jake to take her the night before. She splashed more cold water on her face.

Distress didn't seem to wash off that easily. The lingering image of the child who had appeared toward the end of the dream was even more disturbing. A little boy with Jake's special eyes...Anne compressed her lips. Old pains were very good erasers; so was an intense determination to make sure no child of hers would ever experience the insecurities and instabilities that had marked her own childhood. Hurriedly, she ran a brush through her hair. Last night had been a narrow escape, but she *had* escaped; and she doubted even Jake's ability to conjure up a hot tub in any other campground. In the meantime, she'd seen his whiskered chin and weary eyes.

A few moments later, she removed a steaming cup of coffee from the microwave oven, set it in the console next to Jake, then moved rapidly back to get her own cup. "I'll drive for a while," she called to him. "Just give me a few minutes to get dressed."

"Stop worrying about your clothes and come here."

She brought her cup, vaguely miffed at the order, very definitely startled that the man's attitude this morning so blatantly lacked the lover's seductive skill of the night before, and peered out the window where he motioned. Rather abruptly, she sank down in the passenger seat. The wheat fields, just that quickly, had changed again.

The road ran precariously along a ledge high above a bottomless gorge that yawned threateningly below them. Pink cliffs lined the lonely horizon with strange, contrasting striated lines of crimson and yellow. Pinnacles and buttes jutted up from the gorge below, some shaped like needle-slim knives aimed skyward. In places, the limestone was formed into mystical castles, complete with turrets and waterless moats. In other places, the wind had worn perfect circular holes, caves, or giant mushroom-shaped ledges into the rock. The twisting gorge seemed to gnarl and turn for endless miles; the knifelike peaks stretched high, and the sun streaming onto those desolate rock formations brought out a rainbow spectrum of colors. Pink and blue and green, colors that didn't belong in rock.

"This is one of my favorite places on earth," Jake murmured. He reached for his coffee, glancing only once at her. Through shuttered eyes, he took in the high-necked flannel nightgown, the fair hair loosely coiled over one shoulder, the complexion all rose and cream. Before her nerves could register that intimate perusal, he was turning away. "The Sioux called this land Mako Sica—Bad Land—but they found a harmony with it. The white settlers in such a hurry to get across to find their gold and silver must have called it hell—those that survived."

Anne held her cup in both hands to keep the coffee from spilling as Jake negotiated the twisting uphill road. She immediately decided that this landscape was one of her least favorite places on earth. The land was terrifying, with its gutted hollows and lonely spires. She couldn't imagine how any living thing could survive here. No trees, no water, rock faces too steep to climb; just endless mazes of stone in shadow.

Yet, mesmerized, she couldn't seem to turn away from the window. The colors were incredible, strata of almost bright pink and yellow. The rock formed men and elephants and buildings, and almost any other shape the mind could imagine.

"All kinds of dinosaurs used to romp around here," Jake remarked. "Fox-sized horses and saber-toothed cats, too. Three thousand years ago, nomads hunted this land, finding caves where they could build their fires for the night . . . Would you like to get out?"

Intrigued, she nodded, and set down her cup. When he pulled the motor home to the side of the road, she reached for the door handle.

"Anne?"

She glanced back.

"There's very little chance we'll run into anyone, and it certainly doesn't matter to me. But you might want to put on shoes, honey."

She let go of the door handle as if it were a hot potato. "I was hardly going outside in my nightgown."

"Of course you weren't."

Six and a half minutes later, she emerged flushed and breathless from the back door, wearing a red turtleneck sweater tucked into navy wool culottes, nylons, and a pair of sturdy walking shoes. She had twisted her hair hastily into the untidiest coil she'd ever accomplished in her life, and her makeup consisted only of blusher and lipstick. She was exceedingly pleased with what she'd achieved in six minutes; Jake's responsive chuckle was unnerving. "Break down and tell me the truth, now, Anne. Do you even own a pair of jeans?"

"Where I grew up, you didn't travel in jeans," she said flatly, thoroughly irritated that her appearance didn't pass muster. It was useless to remember that she'd deliberately packed with the thought of playing stiff, formal lady to Jake's devil-may-care vagabond, because at the moment she felt distinctly like a violinist at a rock concert. Truthfully, jeans wouldn't have helped her anyway. She could never fit in here as Jake so easily did, with his hands on denim-clad hips against a backdrop of those jagged peaks, up and down, up and down, like sharp M's across the sky. With his silvery hair and stubborn square chin and rugged profile, Jake could easily have been one of the original pioneers . . . the kind who made it.

He grabbed her hand and pulled her toward a steep rock formation.

"Look," she started unhappily.

"Now don't get all touchy. I love your taste in clothes. I only make fun because you just beg to be teased. Are you wearing the camisole I gave you?"

"I returned it," she snapped through gritted teeth. "I told you that."

"Fib. I saw it buried in your bottom drawer when I was helping you pack—or trying to. You brought it along, didn't you?"

One of Jake's many character flaws was that he thought he knew so much. Anne declined to answer. He started to climb, and she followed silently. The land was veined like old leather, oddly giving beneath her feet, the dusty yellow soil like hard-packed sand but without substance beneath. She reached out and clutched his hand, only because instinct kept telling her that somehow the land wouldn't hold her. Jake moved like an animal, surefooted and silent, leading them into a crevice between two steep rock walls. For Anne, it was a far different kind of exercise than standing in line to buy tickets to a symphony concert.

"Look," Jake said suddenly.

She looked, and backed promptly into the wall of his chest. She was staring at a set of teeth embedded in the rock. *Real* teeth!

"Fossils are all over this route," Jake commented, clearly fascinated by the dental display. He tugged at her hand. "There are a thousand things I'd like to tell you about this place, but we haven't got much time. Idaho's still five hundred miles from here, and I'm determined to get there in the next twenty-four hours. But you have to see this—"

What he evidently wanted her to see was a ledge where one step in the wrong direction could result in an instant plunge of several hundred feet. Wonderful view, Anne thought fleetingly. They seemed to be in hell. Jake's arms draped around her waist and pulled her back against him, providing the only familiar, solid thing to hold on to anywhere in sight. Her eyes skimmed over the scene. Barren cliffs dropped below to a gaunt, lonely terrain of scalloped ridges and mystical shapes. Fire could have raced through this land and never made a difference. Fire, ice, storm . . .

Jake loved this land? She hated it. It was just one more example of the differences between them . . . She suddenly caught sight of a single flower, a purple burst of softness growing from a crack in the rock. Then she had a glimpse of the strange prism of rainbow colors on the cliffs, breathtakingly brilliant hues accented by sun and shade.

Jake's chin nuzzled the crown of her head. "I've heard many stories about this place. A group of people were trying to cross here around a century ago, and they didn't have enough water. They buried two of their party in the sand up to their necks, to preserve what body moisture they had." His arms tightened around her waist. "They survived, Anne, but that's what it took to survive."

She shuddered expressively, leaning back closer against him.

"Then there was an outlaw named Joaquin," Jake drawled. "He hated miners. His bride was Antonia, a sweet, innocent, lovely woman. While he was out one day, a group of miners assaulted his wife. Joaquin was very young, Anne, not more than twenty, and he turned killer after that, killer and thief, with a reputation that surpassed that of any other outlaw in the West." Jake hesitated. "I think of that story every time I come back out here."

An icy chill touched her spine. "Not a very cheerful tale, is it? Thank heavens that kind of thing doesn't happen anymore."

"And we're all civilized now?" Jake shook his head as he slowly turned her around to face him. "You think so, Anne? He was a man alone in a hostile world, who saw only one way to get back at life. I can understand that," he said quietly, holding her closer. "Haven't you ever felt helpless? Powerless to control things that were happening to you? As a little kid, didn't you ever feel rage that people were hurting you and you couldn't stop them?"

"No. Of course not." She slipped quickly from his arms and started the climb down to the motor home. Suddenly, she couldn't get inside the vehicle fast enough. The land was damned. Desolate and hostile, the kind of place that bred outlaws. She wanted her peppermint tea and a twentieth-century chair and a reassuring book about stocks and bonds. She stepped up and into the motor home, out of breath. Only Jake would be demented enough to see a similarity between the feelings of some long-dead outlaw and those of an innocent child.

Some minutes later, Jake silently vaulted into the driver's seat, and they headed back onto the road. After a time, Anne moved up to the passenger seat with a fresh cup of tea warming her hands. She kept as silent as he was. From nowhere, she had a sudden mental image of a five-year-old girl, green-eyed and blond and innocent . . . desperately shaking her most precious doll.

It was the day her dad died, a memory buried so deep she hadn't known it was still there. As a little girl she'd had no idea how to deal with so much anger. *How dare he die, how dare he die, how dare he never hold me again* . . . More images flooded her mind. Marriages, and more marriages, and more marriages. How very adept she'd become at being flower girl at her mother's impulsive weddings. But the image Anne remembered most vividly was of herself hurling pillows and books and pencils. She didn't *want* to go to another school! She'd just made friends at the old one. No one had asked a seven-year-old-child if she wanted to be so joltingly uprooted, if she minded changing schools four more times in the next four years. Boarding school had been Ralph's idea; he was her third stepfather. Her childhood had been a horror of loneliness, a long, disjointed train of *in media res* starts and abrupt finishes and never knowing where anyone was going.

Rage had no place in Anne's adult life; she'd put all that behind her. Everything had changed, anyway, once her grandmother had taken her in. Jennie Blake was stern but loving, a wonderfully strong woman whose home had been a haven. Anne had clung to the stability of household rules and discipline as to a lifeline. There was no more helpless anger. But Jake had touched some very old scars just now, reopened some very deep wounds...

Jake's eyes suddenly flashed to hers, a flicker of dark gray compassion, of the kind of understanding that was just part of Jake. "Maybe I *can* understand your outlaw," she offered quietly.

"I thought you would." He turned back to the road. "You weren't the only one buffeted around as a child, honey."

She averted her eyes, painfully aware of what different roads they'd taken to overcome those uncertain beginnings. "You look tired," she said briskly. "Don't you think it's time I took a turn at the wheel?"

She drove all afternoon. Jake slept in the back of the motor home. And all afternoon, she was haunted by images of his young outlaw. The one who was so very much in love with his innocent, sweet wife. And she thought of Jake, who'd never cared if he had two nickels to rub together... but heaven help anyone who tried to harm anything he *did* care about.

Buttes gave way to steep hills by midafternoon. A huge, low violet cloud ahead of her kept growing larger on the horizon, as the road continued to dip and curve and climb. Only late in the afternoon did she realize that it wasn't a cloud at all, but mountains that reached for

the sky in front of her, snow-peaked and craggy, proud
and royal purple.

"We'll be in the heart of the Bighorns by nightfall."
Jake suddenly yawned from behind her, then moved for-
ward to crouch down on his haunches between the seats.
"Would you believe there's snow predicted in the Big-
horns tonight, yet it'll be seventy degrees tomorrow in
Idaho? That's *west*." He yawned again sleepily. "And
to really get you into the spirit of the land"—he grinned—
"I think I'll serve you yellow-jacket soup by a campfire.
Think you're ready?"

She didn't particularly feel ready for anything. This
strange, unpredictable landscape frightened her, evoked
odd and uncomfortable feelings. Awareness of things she
hadn't thought of in years, didn't really want to think
of . . . yet her eyes were captivated by those mountains,
and she risked a quick glance at Jake after maneuvering
the motor home around a treacherous turn. *"Yellow-jacket
soup*—as in *bees?* Are you out of your mind?"

He was.

Jake drove two forked sticks into the ground, then
took out a pocket knife and started to whittle the bark
off the spit that was to lie between them. The fire, dancing and crackling, was waiting for him. "The thing with
yellow-jacket soup," he said gravely, "is to find the yellow jackets' ground nest when it's full of grubs. And
this is all going to be very difficult to explain if you
don't wipe that cheeky grin off your face."

"I'm so sorry." Anne's eyes flashed merriment. "Most
recipes start with 'Preheat the oven,' but all right, Jake.
Then what?"

"Why do I sense this doubting-Thomas attitude?" Jake
sounded wounded.

"You're imagining it," she assured him.

"How are you coming there?"

"Fine." She was kneading some sort of flour mixture
in a big bowl on her lap, another culinary creation of
Jake's. Which was fine, except that it was snowing. No

big blizzard, but there was no question that the white stuff fluttering down was a little more than falling stars. The cold was seeping through her culottes; it was the biggest, blackest night she'd ever seen; and they were totally alone in a state campground in the Bighorns. Naturally. No one else would be camping—much less cooking out—on a night like this. No one in his right mind.

"Are you ready to hear what else you have to do to make yellow-jacket soup?" Jake demanded.

"I certainly am." The doughy horror was sticking under her fingernails, but she continued kneading. At least the mixture was coating her hands—one way to ward off frostbite.

"You get the grubs off the nest by poking them with a lit match. Then you heat the nest over the fire until it dries out a little. About then you pick off the yellow jackets and cook them separately over the fire; pop them into boiling water, add a little seasoning, and *voilà . . .*"

"Yellow-jacket soup," she applauded. Jake faced her with a level stare as he took the bowl from her hands, removed the dough, and set it in a greased pan near the fire to rise. Anne started laughing helplessly, and pushed up the collar of her coat with her forearms, since her hands were white and sticky.

"It's an *authentic* Indian recipe—"

She started laughing again.

"*—that happens to be quite delectable.*" He clapped her on the back when she started choking.

"Come on, Jake, you've never eaten any such thing in your life!"

"I have, too. Once." He paused, his face taking on a peculiar expression. "God in heaven, once was enough." He rapidly turned toward the fire again. "Nevertheless, you're getting an authentic Indian meal tonight, lady. Just not quite *that* authentic."

"So tell me."

He cast her a sudden critical glance. "Why didn't you tell me you were getting cold?" He hustled her speedily into the motor home, washed the dough off her hands, haphazardly draped her shoulders with a blanket, and covered her hands with a pair of Italian kid gloves he discovered in her purse before hustling her back outside again. Jake gave the gloves a wry look. They were as soft as a baby's bottom, but they wouldn't keep her hands warm even in the tropics. She loved those gloves, though.

When she was settled on the log with the blanket beneath her, he started in again. "First we're having bannock." He motioned to the floury concoction she'd made. After the oddly textured, stiff dough had risen for a few minutes, he stretched it and wrapped it around a stick in coils. "It's a trail bread. You roast it over the fire. No prospector or trailhand or self-respecting Indian would ever have a meal without it. *Very* important."

"Aaah."

He cast her another critical look, though evidently not for that peculiar sound she'd made. Moments later, her head was covered with his orange wool scarf. The fabric chafed her soft cheeks, but it was certainly warm; she just had a sneaking suspicion that the men from the funny farm would find her any minute now. In the orange scarf and blue blanket and cranberry coat, sitting on a log with the mountains all around and the snow lazily drifting down. Worse than that, she was starting to laugh again.

"Then we'll have cactus salad," Jake continued as he turned his back to the fire. "Then Apache-fried rabbit. Only no rabbits happened to have the misfortune of running in front of the motor home. So it's Apache-fried chicken, as it happens. Chicken via the grocery store, but we don't need to mention that—"

"I don't know when you had the time to pick the cactus," she said delicately. Not that she doubted him.

"Well..." Jake sighed. "Once again, we had to veer just a little from our chosen course. The cactus came from a seven-and-a-quarter-ounce can."

"Darling." Anne rarely used casual endearments; this one was necessary to soften the blow. "Cactus doesn't come in a can."

He took a can out of the trash and held it up so that

she could read the label: Natural Cactus in Salt Water, Drain before Using.

"I beg your pardon," she apologized gravely.

"You *persist* in thinking I don't know what I'm doing."

She persisted in thinking nothing of the kind. Jake always knew exactly what he was doing. Her smile faded, just a little. No one but Jake would have made her knead bread dough in the middle of a snowstorm in the Bighorns; no one but Jake had ever elicited purely whimsical laughter from her. She was fascinated by the mountain lore he'd picked up from heaven knew where. Fascinated, happily relieved that she wouldn't have to eat bee soup, and just slightly . . . sad.

Her dark prince had always charmed her, had always created a quiet, intimate, delicious fantasy when just the two of them were together. How could she help reaching out for him? But a lifetime was very different from scattered moments. Sand castles never lasted.

Are you thinking about that boring stuff again? Her emotions warred with her mind. Anne, can't you leave it alone even for a minute?

Jake's eyes sought hers over the crackling fire. The chicken was sizzling on the spit, the bread was browning and the slices of cactus were arranged on two small plates, pimiento slices between them, swimming in a dressing of tarragon-and-pepper-seasoned oil. All of it, unbelievably, looked and smelled quite good.

"You will reserve judgment, Anne, until we've had dinner." His voice was still teasing, but for a moment the humor didn't reach his eyes.

Anne decided to reserve judgment a little longer. The look in his eyes had nothing to do with Apache-fried chicken.

chapter 8

"DELICIOUS, JAKE. I mean it."

Anne had tried the bannock first. The bread was a little tough, oddly sweet, and delectable with melted butter. That had given her the courage to move on to Jake's Apache-fried chicken, and two pieces later she was licking her fingers. The strange batter was fire-sealed and crisp, the meat unbelievably succulent.

"Have another piece." Jake dropped down beside her with a second platter of chicken. The wind was whistling through the cliffs, but at least in their sheltered valley the snow had stopped. Their fire lapped up the darkness, warming their faces and toes...but not their backs. Anne knew her spine was never going to thaw, but at the moment she was hungry for another piece of chicken...

A sterling silver fork, utterly incongruous in this wilderness, suddenly made its way in front of her nose. As Jake dangled a forkful of cactus salad before her, Anne swallowed. "Listen, Jake, it's not that I don't want to try your salad. I've grown cactus in my kitchen, you know; I *like* cactus. Which is why it occurred to me that maybe the Indians might have found an edible variety.

Particularly if they were suffering from absolute starvation—"

Since her mouth was unfortunately open, Jake took advantage and inserted a sliver of the pale green cactus between her lips. It tasted like a smooth, mild avocado— not at all what she was expecting. "Good?" he asked.

She took the plate from his hands. "If I answer that, I'll never hear the end of the I-told-you-so's. You think I was born yesterday?"

"I told you—" With exacting precision, she aimed a forkful of chicken at his wagging tongue, and chuckled at his response.

"You're looking for trouble," he suggested.

Actually, she wasn't, not just then. As rapidly as she was devouring the salad on her plate, Jake was forking cactus bits to her from his own, knowing her fondness for anything that even vaguely resembled an avocado.

"Are you cold?" he asked suddenly.

"Freezing. Don't take that away," she protested when he started to rise with the chicken platter.

He set it back down. "I'm beginning to think you've never been on a cookout before," he said, amused.

"You know darn well I haven't. It's a mystery to me how people could do this for recreation. The fire, for instance. Your toes burn while your back freezes. Your fingers get sticky, which means sooner or later everything else gets sticky. At least it's too cold for bugs, but I'm afraid to take my eyes off the woods for fear a bear or cougar will come lumbering down for its dinner. This is supposed to be competition for a restaurant with soft lighting and Irish linen and inside plumbing?"

"Anne?"

Her eyelashes flashed up, shadowing spikes on her cheeks in the firelight. How had his face loomed close so suddenly? She could smell him, all pine and cold freshness. "I hate to have to tell you this, honey, but you're having a wonderful time." Jake dropped a kiss on her forehead that reeked of satisfaction, readjusted his scruffy wool scarf rather possessively around her ears, and started cleaning away their debris.

A wistful expression touched her features with softness. *Yes,* darn him, she was having a perfectly wonderful time. This rough-and-tumble life was her idea of torture, but for a few special hours... The word *lonely* surged into her mind from nowhere; loneliness was an emotion they always banished when they were together.

Rising to help, she found herself watching Jake. While she brought their few plates and silverware into the motor home, he put out the fire. He was a very fussy man. By the time he was done, there wasn't a sign that anyone had been near their cooking site.

The wind seemed to have pushed every last cloud out of the sky, and now a silver moon cast its pale glow on the tall pines. Anne draped the blanket closer around her, waiting for Jake. He'd made fun of himself for buying the chicken from the grocery store, but every movement he made said that he was a survivor, well used to the wilderness. His rugged features caught shadow, then light; his spine was always straight, his step silent. Was he lonely, too? she wondered fleetingly. She didn't at all like the thought of Jake being lonely. His eyes suddenly captured hers.

"Would you kindly get your cold toes inside the motor home?" he scolded her.

"Yours have to be just as cold." But he hurried her inside ahead of him, and slammed the door, leaving all the cold outside. They kept getting in each other's way, taking off their coats and gloves and putting everything away. Anne started running water in the sink to wash their dishes, but Jake nudged her aside, which was just as well. He'd bunched the blankets up and dropped them in a heap, and she would have to refold them all. Once a picture-straightener, always a picture-straightener, she thought idly, but that wasn't at all what was really on her mind.

"Isn't it funny, Jake," she said casually, "how you turned out to be wind and I turned out to be stone? We both started out so very much the same. Your parents were together when you were small, but you were jostled about just as much as I was. Different schools, different houses, all that." She hesitated, then brushed past him to put away the neatly folded blankets. For a moment, she hid her face from him, her fingers—for no reason at all—clutching at the soft wool. "It just seems strange how very different we turned out. You've never even had the first urge to stay in one place, have you?"

Her tone was light. *Don't worry, Jake, I don't care. I would never try to change you. I just thought I would ask, one time, if you could conceivably ever ever ever ever settle down . . .*

His fingers suddenly curled around her shoulders, turning her to face him. To Anne, his eyes had never seemed as silver, as liquid, as they did at that moment. "I never could seem to care where I hung my hat," he said quietly, "and I doubt that I ever will, Anne. Do you want me to lie to you?"

She shook her head. "Never."

"I've been on the move a long while." His thumb gently traced the line of her cheekbone. "And lonely, many times. But there's excitement and challenge and a freshness about new ideas and new people, new worlds. So much to know and share and see. A *place* to you means safety, honey, but I've never been able to really believe that. That you can feel *safe* simply because you stay in just one place. And I won't make you a promise I can't keep."

His lips touched down, cool and firm on hers. Her hands fingered the soft flannel of his sleeve, then moved up to his neck, drawing him closer, drawing in his kiss. She had her answer. Jake knew he wouldn't change. And Anne knew *she* wouldn't. So Jake was a rolling stone who couldn't change his ways, but she'd always known that, deep down. Yet her kiss was one of hunger, of loneliness, of wanting to blot out the answer he'd given her.

His lips brushed hers once more, then lifted. A fingertip gently traced the line of her lower lip, slow and sensual. Brooding eyes searched hers. "You're so damned sure that matters."

She groped for an answer as honest as his own words, but a sudden playful tap on her backside startled her. "To bed with you. And to make absolutely sure you go alone, I'm going to hit the road again."

She blinked, then frowned. "Jake, you've already pushed yourself too hard. You started driving this morning at two o'clock."

"Stopping on the road wastes too much time," he said. "I couldn't be less tired." There was no talking to him. Minutes later, she heard him start the engine. Anne took down her coil of hair and started brushing it. With the lights off in back, she curled up in the chair, welcoming the darkness as her brush worked vigorously until her scalp tingled and her hair was silken-smooth. She couldn't seem to get rid of the feeling that she'd disappointed him. How very easy it would have been to tell him that she didn't care where they went or how often they moved as long as they were together. She might have said that to him when she was eighteen. At thirty-one, that kind of lie really wasn't possible. She knew all too well what was really important to her.

An hour later, she crawled into the upper berth and fell asleep.

"Wake up, up there, sleepyhead. I have a present for you."

"Go away," Anne mumbled. It was a night and a morning later, and between the two of them they'd driven almost the entire time. For more than half of the ride, they'd been on Highway 90, a road that apparently never ended, although Jake kept claiming it would eventually lead them to Idaho. The Silver Valley was obviously one of his pipe dreams. All she'd seen so far was Montana's endless buttes and pale yellow grasses and infinite barren sky . . . and Jake's quiet, very determined profile. She'd had enough of all of them.

The motor home slowed and then came to a stop.

Anne paid no attention, snuggling the comforter over her head. A tiny swirl of cool air gusted under the covers at her feet. She'd never minded cold toes... but the soft lap of a smooth tongue on her instep was another matter.

She murmured a lecture on repression into the pillow. Strong teeth nibbled at her toes; she shifted her foot, appalled. Then two rough, distinctly male fingertips started walking up her heel, over her slim ankle and curved calf, to the back of her ticklish knee, chasing her nightgown up her thigh... Anne sleepily opened her eyes and peeked out from under the covers.

"One more inch and it's Death Valley days for you," she threatened groggily.

"The lady even wakes up sassy," Jake marveled. "Which is the question. *Is* the lady awake?"

"No." She pulled the comforter over her head again. "Where are we?"

"In Idaho. That means no more sleeping for you, honey." Jake sounded sympathetic; his actions certainly weren't. He tugged mercilessly at her comforter until it tumbled down to the carpet behind the driver's seat. Anne tried to curl into a tight ball, but his fingers closed over one ankle, then the other. "Now, Anne. I didn't want to do this the hard way—"

"Would you kindly have the courtesy to take a long, fast hike, like out into the middle of the Atlantic Ocean!"

"Now, Anne," he repeated, tugging at both ankles while she frantically pushed her nightgown back down, starting to laugh helplessly as she batted at his hands. It was like wrestling with a soft-pawed bear who just kept coming at her. He won, naturally, solely because of his brawn. In a confusion of nightgown and tousled hair swirling around her face and tickling fingers and Jake's laughing eyes, she finally felt her toes touch the carpet, forsaking the wonderfully warm berth. "Boiling in oil would be too good—" she started to say.

But she didn't finish. Something had happened to the laughter in his eyes, in the pressing of her body to his, in the kiss that came out of nowhere.

"You smell like sleep. All warm and snuggled up and cuddly," he murmured. His palms were splayed on her bottom, drawing her deliberately against his thighs, raising her blood pressure unexpectedly. He'd made it more than clear he had no intention of making love to her on the road, and Anne was increasingly bewildered by his continued restraint. They had only two weeks...

She reached up to touch his rough-bearded cheek. "You look terrible," she informed him sleepily. "Darn it, Jake, why are you driving yourself so hard?" Her lips followed in the wake of her hand, until she snuggled closer for a simple, unavoidable, unexplainable, delicious hug. His chamois shirt was soft and his body warm, and when his arms wrapped around her she felt sleepy all over again, defenseless, not caring... It was far too early in the morning to think about principles and problems.

Jake's thighs tightened responsively against her softer ones. His fingers threaded back her hair as he dipped down to kiss her just behind her ear. "Don't you want to see Idaho?" he questioned.

"No."

"Don't you want to see your present? Actually, there are two."

"No."

In slow motion, his hands weaved down under her hair. His fingers, cloaked by the heavy tresses, moved over her shoulders, then down her spine, then lower to cup her bottom again, molding the shape of him to her own shape. Her pulse was beating erratically. She wanted to sing. She was weary of traveling and weary of worrying, and undoubtedly when she really woke up, her head would overrule all the base impulses that were racing through her bloodstream. She could deal with that later. Right now, the silver eyes that captured hers promised that Jake was very much of like mind, full of base, unprincipled, degenerate thoughts.

"Although," he said gently, "we are parked on the edge of a cliff."

"That's nice." But unwillingly she shifted her eyes away from him to the window. The nose of the motor home really did seem to be hanging in midair. At least all she could see was a terrifying drop below to a tree-studded valley where pines of gold and green reached valiantly for the sky. *Gold pines?* Her heart flipped over, in an entirely different realm. "What happened to the grassy plains?"

"They turned into Idaho."

"Pines are supposed to stay green all year, not turn gold like that."

"Idaho pines don't follow the rules," he agreed. "It's also already warm outside. Not quite as warm as inside, I'll grant you..." He drew away from her with a distinctly crooked smile. "But I'm beginning to have the feeling this day could turn out very warm indeed."

He didn't seem to be talking about the weather. As Jake went back to the driver's seat, Anne groped for clothes and padded back to the bathroom, feeling curiously light-headed. She felt less so when he'd backed away from the cliff and was safely on the highway again. She washed and drew on underthings, occasionally peeking out the curtained window in back.

In the Bighorns, there had been snow. How strange to look out and see mountains here that looked even taller, yet totally different. These spiky peaks were tall and skinny and steep, too steep for a house to be set anywhere, too steep for any other road to have been built, and there were no other roads that she could see. Just the one highway. And the crazy gold pines...there had to be millions of them, all catching the warm sunlight's glint and shimmer. Clouds lay right on the road, like wisps of cotton candy. They were driving so high up she could feel her ears pop...

She slipped on stockings, skirt, and blouse, then started working impatiently with her hair. Her mirror image annoyed her. The coral Victorian blouse was a favorite, with its splash of lace at her throat and wrists, and the camel-colored skirt fit well, gathered just a little around her slim hips. The outfit was tailored and trim and feminine . . . and totally wrong. It had once seemed terribly important to show Jake she wasn't the jeans and sweat shirt type and never would be, but she could at least have had the sense to be a bit less stubborn and more practical. One pair of pants wouldn't have killed her.

Her fingers hesitated, forming the tight coil at the back of her neck. Impulsively, she loosened the confining knot, allowing a few strands to curl around her ears. The effect was not particularly practical. Or sensible. She turned away from the mirror.

A few minutes later, she carried two mugs of coffee up to the front of the motor home, setting both down as she noticed two packages on the rug between the seats. Her eyebrows flickered up in question.

"I told you I had presents for you this morning."

"I thought you were joking. Jake, I don't want you to buy—"

"These are arriving-in-Idaho presents. They're necessities," he assured her.

"Necessities?" she echoed faintly as she sank down into the passenger seat. The first package was tiny, wrapped in silver paper with a huge satin pink bow. "Jake," she started to scold, but stopped when she saw the exquisite filigree of silver inside, a necklace so delicate and light she was afraid to touch it.

"Do you like it?"

"I . . . it's beautiful. More than beautiful." She looked at him helplessly.

He nodded. "It suits a woman who wears lace at her throat and soft colors next to her skin." He took a quick inventory, and she could have sworn at that moment he was pleased at her choice of dress. "Now open the other package, Anne—but be careful. It's heavy."

She took another moment to finger the necklace, and then on impulse put it on and fastened its tiny catch behind her neck. "Jake, it's so . . ." She hesitated, an odd tremor in her voice, and then leaned over to kiss his cheek. "Thank you."

"You're welcome."

The other package was the shape of a brick, and when Anne bent to lift it she couldn't. She arched both eyebrows in Jake's direction, but he didn't turn away from the road. Cautiously, she undid the wrappings—and then froze.

"It weighs about seventy pounds, honey. A really effective paperweight." He hesitated, adding sadly, "You can be hard to buy for, sometimes. But I figured this was something you could really use when you get busy pushing papers around."

The silver ingot was the size of a brick, a solid block of gleaming metal so bright, so mirror-bright, that the sun reflecting off it hurt Anne's eyes.

"First," Jake said lazily, "we're going to mine a little silver. Then we'll head up to my ghost town, Anne, where I usually set up camp when I'm here. *Not* where I have in mind your living with me, but we'll get to Coeur d'Alene in a day or two." He paused. "Actually, we might stop off and put that little ingot in a bank vault while we travel around. I have to admit it's made even me a little nervous to have it just lying around . . ."

If Anne had *known* it had been "just lying around," she would have developed an ulcer. As it was, she stared down at the ingot with a disbelieving expression.

"Jake, you're out of your mind. Stark raving out of your mind."

chapter 9

ANNE TURNED SILENT, once Jake came back out of the bank and started driving through the narrow streets of Wallace. The touch and look of the silver ingot was indelibly engraved in her mind, evoking unwilling fantasies of sterling castles ... and a dreadful anxiety as to exactly what Jake had got himself involved in.

The look of the town was just not what she'd expected. Jake had been playing tourist guide, blithely relating that Idaho's Silver Valley produced more than 40 percent of the nation's metal ores. Wallace, he said, was the unofficial capital of the valley. He went on about geological fault lines and mineral deposits and the incredible wealth hidden in the mountains. Anne was hardly the type to whimsically imagine streets lined with silver, but Wallace ... well.

The town was about as big as a handkerchief, and appeared as old as the hills behind it. SILVER SHARES SOLD HERE shouted the signs in every other window. So much wealth in gold and silver, pocketed in this tiny, tiny place? The mountains simply didn't provide growing room. Old frame structures were packed one on top of the other. Houses had backyards that led to a second tier of houses, with steps that led to a third tier of houses— and beyond that the mountains shot straight up.

"Not what you expected, Anne?"

"I can picture it as a rough, tough western town about a hundred years ago," she admitted.

"She hasn't changed. She's known gunfights, fire, feast, and famine, and I don't think anything ever will change her. Not as long as there's silver in the hills."

Yes. His silver. Anne took a breath, intrigued by Jake's town but not at all by his latest business venture. "Jake, I *wish* you hadn't got into this. You think I know nothing about the commodities market? The price of silver has fluctuated like crazy in the last few years. It's a game of futures, where a broker contracts to buy or sell lots at a set price at some future date. The investors purchase those futures with margin money and go long or short—"

"I love it when you talk money," Jake drawled. "Did you know that in India they serve silver-roasted chickens at weddings? They actually eat the stuff."

"So," Anne said crisply, "the sucker speculator agrees to buy silver at so many dollars an ounce in, say, three months. Or four. Or whatever. That's all fine and good for him if the price per ounce is higher when that time comes; that means he gets more silver than he paid for. But if the price is *lower,* Jake, you have to put up more margin money."

"It's like listening to the flow of Greek," Jake remarked to the world in general.

"Silver is a perfectly insane commodity to become involved in. How's that for plain English?"

Jake shook his head. "Now let's not get violent, honey. I didn't buy futures. I bought the *mines.*"

"Oh, *Lord.*"

"You see, I found dozens of little mines that had been closed down for years. The silver in those mines wasn't top-grade metal. But when demand for silver went sky high, I decided to go for it. You see, by themselves those little mines might not have been profitable, but put them all under one roof—*my* roof—and it's a whole different ball game . . . Where are you going?"

"To get some antacid tablets. I can't take this."

The motor home didn't stock antacid tablets. Anne settled for peppermint tea.

"Listen," she started tactfully, as she carried her cup forward and sat down again. Only she couldn't seem to continue. Jake pulled into a gas station, passed the pumps, and drove straight through onto another road. A road of sorts. The asphalt abruptly led straight up, like the start of a roller-coaster ride. Anne's tea splashed, and her head bumped against the seat's headrest. Before she could catch her breath, they were headed into a hairpin turn.

There were no guard rails along the side of the road. That was unfortunate, because there was a three-hundred-foot drop between the road and the valley below. If she'd had the urge, she could have opened the window and patted the tops of the tallest pines she had ever seen in her life. She didn't have the urge.

"Jake—"

"We're headed for the first mine I ever saw in this area. A really tiny one, actually, with no major tunnels or caverns. You've always been a little claustrophobic, and I didn't think you'd want to go a thousand feet down inside the earth."

"You've got *that* right," Anne affirmed.

Jake chuckled. "So I thought I'd break you in nice and easy . . . You'd better drink that tea while you can," he suggested.

Anne agreed. She sipped the scalding liquid as if it were fortified with courage. They were going to die on that road. Soon. The steep upgrade suddenly became a steep downgrade. The vehicle hit sixty—and that with Jake's foot on the brake. "Most people only think of silver in terms of jewelry and flatware," he informed her casually. "I've got one mine that produces a grade high enough for these things, but the others—"

Anne moaned. "Exactly how many mines do you own?"

"I sell the rest of my silver to various industries. Medicine, for one. Orthopedic surgeons use a cement containing silver salts to mend damaged bones. Did you know that? And patients who've been burned badly need silver, too . . . I've always had this horror of being burned. Without a silver cream to disinfect the burns—"

"Jake." Anne set down her empty cup and clutched the arm rest. *"Where* is this mine? How far from here?"

"Just a little way. What's wrong?"

"Nothing." The roller coaster was going up again, curling around like a rattlesnake. The treetops were about five hundred feet below now. A jeep was hurtling toward them from the opposite direction. Anne closed her eyes.

"And then there's California, Anne. It can get pretty dry in certain parts of California. Silver can be chemically altered to form silver iodide crystals, and they can be used to seed the clouds—to *make rain,* Anne, for people who desperately need it. One thirtieth of an ounce of silver can yield ten trillion ice crystals."

"That's absolutely wonderful."

Her palms were embarrassingly damp—which wouldn't have been at all embarrassing if Jake hadn't reached out and claimed one. "I've driven this road at night in the rain, honey."

"Then you have a death wish."

"There's nothing to worry about."

Which was exactly where they parted ways philosophically. She knew very clearly when there was something to worry about. Jake had never worried about anything in his life. "How often do you have to drive this road?" she asked, very casually.

"Every day during the week. Well . . ." He paused. "I've spent more time near Coeur d'Alene lately. You could tell from the look of Wallace that there's really no place to live there, no space. You'll love the place where I park the motor home, Anne. You won't want to love it, but you will." He paused again. "I haven't finished telling you about silver."

She listened, desperate to keep her mind on anything but the logging truck that suddenly loomed ahead of them. Their motor home was on the inside curve, but the huge vehicle had rattling logs in its bed... She bit her lip as the logger whizzed past them. The taste of blood was sweet and warm.

"*Film*, Anne. An ounce of silver is all it takes to make five thousand color photographs. I've just started selling to film manufacturers. Like the buyers for every other industry, they require a specific grade of silver. And that's just the point. I've got lots of different mines, so I can provide several different grades to different buyers. No other metal conducts as well as silver, and it's a natural dry lubricant... You can open your eyes now," Jake said mildly.

She did. Jake vaulted outside to open a tall, weathered wooden gate with a No Trespassing sign nailed to it. The killer road was behind them, replaced by a gravel lane. Once they were inside the gate, they might as well have entered another world. The mountain valley was flat, a grassy field leading to a stand of gold pines, backdropped by the spiked hills.

When Jake stopped the vehicle and turned the key, Anne stepped out and took a good long breath. The sun beat down in warm, soothing rays, as if apologizing for that harrowing ride. Fresh, sweet air surged into her lungs, and at the same time curiosity was battering questions in her head. *This* little dale was mining country? "Jake?" She turned to see Jake stepping out from the back of the motor home, with a pair of decrepit black galoshes in his hand.

"Anne, I stuffed socks in the toes so they'd fit you. There's no way you're going into the mine with heels on."

"*What* mine?"

"Baby Rivard." He motioned. She saw nothing but a grove of trees, and then the fluff of a rabbit's tail as it hopped away from them. Her eyes skimmed back to the grin on Jake's face, and the permanently muddy boots in his hands. With a wry smile, she exchanged her Italian leather sandals for his choice of footwear.

He took her hand as they started walking toward the face of the cliff. The boots felt cold and clammy on her stockinged feet, and no one would have considered them graceful. Only when they'd passed through the grove of trees did she see the planks that formed a path to the opening of a cave.

"This mine won't ever be profitable, Anne. The vein's shallow and not worth the effort of taking out the ore, but it will give you a good idea what a silver mine really looks like. Almost all silver comes from ores that contain larger amounts of other metals. Lead, usually, and copper a lot of the time. This little honey's got copper and gold and quartz. The ore's rich—it's where I got the silver your necklace is made from—but it yields only a few ounces of silver for every ton of ore. That's why..."

Jake stepped into the dark hollow in the mountain, still holding Anne's hand. As she followed him, she shivered suddenly in the cold, dank air. He released her hand and took a lantern from a hook. She watched him light it and hold it high so that they could see the passageway ahead of them.

"Are you listening, Anne?"

"Yes." She was listening, though not entirely to the lecture on silver. She was listening to a side of Jake she'd never heard before. Nothing in heaven or on earth could convince her that silver would provide a practical, stable livelihood, but for the moment that wasn't the point. For a man who had roamed lackadaisically from one project to another all his life, Jake clearly had learned a great deal about Idaho... and silver.

He'd changed, she thought fleetingly. Or had she misunderstood the man in the past? She watched his face, so full of animation, his silvery eyes picking up the flickering reflections from the lantern's light. She couldn't possibly follow everything he was talking about. "They

grind it into dust . . . loosen it from the rock, submerge
it in tanks of foaming water . . . Tailings . . . ash-gray
sludge . . . then the refinery process . . ." He was really
irresistibly handsome, all shoulders in the chamois shirt,
all lithe grace and tawny head and sheer brazen male
every time he moved.

Finally, Jake stopped leading her through the laby-
rinthine passageway with its floor of small, gritty rocks.
"There." He motioned.

Her eyes were reluctantly diverted from his profile to
the strange walls of the cave. She'd been so busy, between studying Jake and trying to keep from stumbling
on the uneven ground, that she had really barely looked
at their surroundings.

Moisture dripped slowly down the rough, craggy walls.
When Jake lifted the lantern just so, the inside of his
mountain took on color—the greenish gleam of copper,
the translucent sheen of marble, the threads of pale yellow, and last—and brightest—a long streak of pure silver.

"If there were lead in the vein, the silver would have
shown up as black. That's why I wanted you to see it
pure, Anne."

Tentatively, she reached out to touch the gleaming
vein. The cave was dark and damp and claustrophobic . . . but the silver thread beneath her fingers felt soft,
smooth, and uniquely alive. Its pure beauty didn't belong
here at all. Unwillingly, she felt Jake's enthusiasm suddenly catch up with her. Not that she would ever ever
become involved in anything so foolhardy . . .

Jake hung the lantern on a hook in the cave's ceiling
and turned Anne to face him, capturing the fingers that
had been slowly following the silver vein. "You're catching it, aren't you?" he murmured. Laughter was in his
eyes, laughter . . . and something else. He pulled her arms
around his neck and leaned down to touch his forehead
to hers. "Silver fever. Not the greed *for* it, but the fascination *with* it. And the treasure's there, Anne; it's always been there, all through these mountains for centuries.

Some men have captured it, but most have failed. It's just too hard to reach." His voice changed. "Some love affairs follow that same course. The woman is the treasure, yet how elusive she's been through the years. Self-contained, her vulnerable core well hidden. No one's keeping count of the number of men who've tried to claim her. It doesn't matter. They haven't been smart enough to outwit the lady, now, have they?"

Anne shook her head, suddenly feeling shaky. "Jake—"

"We're only talking about silver, Anne. And mountains. Relax." He tipped her face up, and lowered his lips to hers, pulling her into the promise of riches he offered. Not silver, not metals, not wealth, but adventure and softness and wild, wild dreams.... Her fingers got lost in the thick texture of his hair, splaying on his scalp, pulling him closer. She rose up on tiptoe in the oversized boots; the silky Victorian blouse molded ever so willingly to his chest.

A kiss intended as a moment's sharing seemed to change its mind. Jake's arms tightened on her back, moving slowly down the supple shape of her. She no longer felt the chill of the cave. Silver was running in her veins. Molten silver, smooth and hot and shiny. And suddenly Jake was kissing her again, over and over, rough, drugging kisses...

Her hands traced the feel of sinew and flesh, from his neck to his spine to the small of his back. As though some wanton fire had bewitched them, her fingers tightened on his hips, inviting the intimacy, deliberately provocative. *Your silver scares me, Jake*, her heart whispered. *but don't you dare share your crazy dreams with anyone else*.

So slowly his lips lifted from hers, his eyes never leaving her face. His profile would have looked jagged and harsh if those eyes hadn't been filled with the same warm wanting as her own. "No more waiting, Anne," he said quietly.

It was very definitely a statement, not a question. She

couldn't pretend not to know what he was talking about. He smoothed back her hair, his expression grave.

The touch of his palm was suddenly possessive and disturbing. She reached for his wrist and dragged his hand down to his side. "You know more about futures and margins than I do, don't you, Jake? Yet you let me talk on and on."

A spark of humor glinted in his eyes. They both relaxed. "Now, Anne. I never—"

"Don't you *now, Anne* me. You've done an outstanding job over the years of presenting yourself as devil-may-care, move-on-a-whim Jake, never staying anywhere long enough to get deeply involved in anything."

"I did that?" He made the effort to look surprised. "Maybe the lady was always a little too serious. Maybe it was fun to incite her to laughter, to shock her just a little." He reached up for the lantern. "And keeping in character, honey, I think it's time we hit my ghost town."

His ghost town was perfectly awful.

Anne stood with hands on slim hips, staring in all directions around her. The drive from the mine to here hadn't taken long, just twenty minutes of suicidal hairpin turns—she was getting used to those—and then a cow path behind another fence. A steel fence this time, marked well and locked. Anne pivoted to face him. "You actually live here for weeks at a time?" she questioned casually.

Jake, his hands lazily jammed into his jeans pockets, had found a shady chestnut to lean against, out of the hot sun. His face was in shadow, though she knew he was watching her. "This is where I generally set up the motor home, yes. Weekends I drive the jeep back and forth to Coeur d'Alene, and during the week when I can, but it's not always possible." He paused. "Rugby was the name of this town. It lived and died all within the decade of the 1890's. About the 1920's there was a short revival. Didn't last long." Jake gestured. "I own the whole town, from that crag"—he gestured again—"to that peak."

Her heart sank. Perhaps unconsciously Anne had been praying for a miracle, a place she could live in, particularly after realizing that Jake was seriously committed to his silver.

The meadow was lovely. Lush, low grasses whispered in the sun. The town was high . . . so high that the pure air almost hurt her lungs, so high that the tree-softened peaks on all sides of their private little valley seemed part of the sky. Clouds were touchably close. A gurgling stream rushed near her feet, the sun glinting clearly on its stone bed, and aspens clustered near Jake's chestnut tree. Their leaves were tinged with gold and fluttered even without a breeze, showing off their gilded decorations.

It was almost a magical place, and the three structures standing in the distance only added to that mystical quality. As ghost towns went, this was no metropolis. One of the frame structures housed Jake's jeep. The other two were as old and as ghostly and deserted as the rest of the town. Both were two-story frame buildings, with wildflowers clustered near their doors, creeping over the windows as if they had slowly but surely decided to hide the buildings completely, along with their owners' secrets. Anne itched to explore, to get inside the buildings and imagine what it must have felt like to be the wife of a miner, to know that her dreams depended on the secrets of those mountains . . .

Reality was knowing it was forty miles down to the corner grocery store—forty miles down that killer road. Neighbors, schools, culture—even a drive-in-movie—simply weren't. The water from the stream was undoubtedly pure and delicious, if one wanted to lug buckets of it from the stream to the house. Electricity might reach the area in the next century. The landscape was lovely, yes, and ideal for a nature girl who delighted in stepping outside in the morning to say hello to her friendly local bear. Or cougar. Or wolf. Very nice.

Anne knew she couldn't live here in a thousand years.

chapter 10

JAKE DRAPED AN arm over her shoulder, brushing a kiss on the crown of her head. "You like my ghost town?"

"It's beautiful. Like a corner of the world no one has ever seen. I can see why you love it, Jake. The peace and privacy..."

His chin nuzzled the top of her head. "Now let's *not* panic until we see Coeur d'Alene, shall we?"

Anne stiffened. "I wasn't *panicking,*" she protested. "If you want to spend the rest of our two weeks here, it's fine with me. *Really* it is, Jake..."

"You're fibbing." He turned her slowly to face him, and locked her in a loose embrace with his arms on her shoulders. "Know how I can tell? Even when you tell a little white lie, that pulse in your throat works like a jackhammer."

Perhaps. Anne flashed him a rueful smile that gradually died. She could feel a different mood sweep over both of them, like the tick of a clock in the night. Jake was close, more than close. The sun was bearing down on both of them, and she could smell the sweet grasses and tangy pines, and Jake, the warmth of him. His eyes held wanting, and his finger slowly touched the errant pulse in her throat. "A few days here and there . . . you'd like Idaho on that basis, Anne. Not to romp and stomp like a weekend backpacker, but because you—like me— need a haven from time to time. I didn't buy this particular piece of land for its silver, or its real-estate value. I bought it for its silence. But as for living here permanently—you don't need to lie. You've never needed to lie—not to me."

"I thought . . . it mattered to you," she said gently.

He shook his head. "I've been trying to tell you for a very long time that there's only one thing that matters to me." His look said, *You, Anne.* She closed her eyes, feeling his fingers ever so gently thread through the loose coil at the nape of her neck as his mouth came down on hers. His lips tasted so sweet, so warm and smooth. She heard his indrawn breath against her mouth as her long silken tresses cascaded into his hands. The lightheaded feeling that surged through her was partly real and partly a lush feminine fantasy taking on life. Jake seemed to catch fire when her hair was unbound.

The caution of years slipped from her. Her hands swept over his hard forearms and shoulders, memorizing them. Bittersweet emotions reverberated in her soul. She'd come with him . . . to find answers she already knew. A place she couldn't live in, a lifestyle she just couldn't accept . . . and feelings that just wouldn't die. Her fingers shifted to the front of his shirt. One by one, the buttons loosened. Her lips touched down, each time; first on his throat, then in the curling mat of hair on his chest, then over his heartbeat . . .

"Anne," Jake murmured.

She paid no attention. Jake was new each time; that was part of it. Never mind that they'd known each other intimately before; he was still new to her, all over again. Every single time, she was surprised at the breadth of shoulder, at the haphazard spray of hair on his chest, at muscles that never showed beneath his clothes, at ribs that led down to a ridiculously lean waist; she had wider

hips than he did, though she was slim. His flesh turned
warm under her fingertips; that always surprised her.

He captured her wandering hands, forced them around
his neck, and his lips sealed hers with fierce, delicious
pressure. She nearly drowned before he let her up for
air. "You're in a hell of a lot of trouble, Anne," he
informed her huskily.

Now *that* she'd known from the day they'd met. A
faint smile touched her lips as she lifted her face. How
could it possibly be so hot on an autumn day? Sunlight
washed over Jake's jagged, familiar features, for a moment mesmerizing her. He was working the buttons at
the back of her blouse, one by one. Silently, she reached
up to unfasten the tiny clasp of the silver necklace, and
folded the precious gift carefully into the pocket of his
chamois shirt. She took extra care as she pushed the shirt
from his shoulders. In a moment, her blouse joined his
shirt on the grass, and the sun stroked warmth on her
bare shoulders.

She was vaguely aware that they were standing in an
open meadow. She even tried to mention the fact, but
Jake's lips sealed hers to silence. His sweet, silken tongue
claimed the intimacy of her mouth, all the sensitive dark
corners. The taste—Jake's taste—was a drug, different
from any other drug. She rose up on tiptoe, as his fingers
unclasped her bra, roughly removed it, and so very gently,
so very possessively, claimed one swelling orb in his
hand. Her sanity slipped another notch. Her breathing
changed; one heartbeat became two, then three. Oddly
confused, she buried her lips in his shoulder, and felt a
slow, hot shudder possess his body.

"Anne," he warned hoarsely.

So, Jake, too, was suddenly aware they were outside—not a convenient place at all, not at all what either
of them had intended. Yet a sudden thread of desperation
laced through her bloodstream. Never to touch him again?
Never to *know* him again? Anne, being Anne, knew this
was the precise time to buy a plane ticket for home. So
obviously it must be someone else unbuckling Jake's

well-worn belt, pulling it through the loops on his jeans . . .

His hands made a game of slowly chasing her skirt down over her silk-clad hips, then slowly pushing the half-slip down, then her stockings and panties, and then there was nothing to chase but flesh, and he played that game, too. By the time they were both naked, years seemed to have passed, years of playing those languid, lazy games. Anne's knees felt weak; it was so much easier to sink down.

The long, tall grass yielded beneath her weight, making a strange bed; a silky blouse for a pillow, crinkling jeans under her back, sun-warmed earth and grass beneath her calves. Sunlight flashed in front of her eyes, and the flickering gold leaves of the trees. Jake's face, grainy and tan, was just above her, his eyes savoring the fevered brilliance in hers, the slight trembling of her mouth, the glow of sun and desire that seemed to heat her skin. "I could look at you forever," he murmured.

But he seemed to have sweeter tortures in mind. Slowly, he rained light kisses along her ribs and navel and the inside of her arm, the underside of her chin, settling finally on the hollow between her breasts. The creamy globes were swollen, aching, waiting, and her whole body trembled when his tongue lapped first at one nipple, then the other.

She stroked his length in turn. Slowly. Her fingernails lightly scored his skin; then her gentle hands kneaded the flesh of his shoulders, his back, lower. Her fingertips could reach the backs of his thighs if she arched her whole body just so, if she moved her lips just so, if she flattened her breasts against his male breasts, nipple to nipple . . .

Jake sucked in breath he never seemed to let out again, his mouth hovering over hers. "Anne." His kiss was hard and almost rough, and then there was another, and another. "If by some remote chance you're harboring a hope that we're going to make it to the motor home . . ."

A terrible idea. She eased one leg between his in answer, sealing him closer. The sun made her eyes ache,

and she closed them. Urgency seemed suddenly to claim
them both. Their mattress of jeans and silk was gone;
they were rolling over and over in the grass, grass that
smelled so sweet, that tickled them as it crackled and
yielded under their weight. She seemed to be a part of
the earth, giving and warm, rich and fertile. Somewhere
nearby was the gurgling stream, and the sun kept beating
down...

He took her, a sharp, welcome intrusion into the most
private part of Anne; she wrapped her legs around him;
her fevered green eyes were intense on his. The power
of her own feelings frightened her; her need and love
for this man were open, she was suddenly aware of the
impermanence of their love, the illusiveness of their future. Then his lips captured hers, locking out the bitter
and leaving only the sweet.

She'd made love with him before; it had been glorious,
yet never like this, like a strong wind that would have
its way, all the wild, fierce rush of a storm, all the
gentleness of a breeze. Jake was so tender, teasing her
higher, and all around her were the crushed grasses and
the smells of autumn and sun and earth. The sensations
seemed magnified, sweet and primitive, special. Then
they were gone; there was only Jake; the world could
have been spinning in circles; she knew only Jake. Desire
ripped through her like a sharp, desperate pain, a rhythm
gone too far to stop, a ruby-red promise of something
she so frantically needed and could never have named
or asked for...

The sun exploded in front of her eyes.

She held on to Jake, shuddering, gradually aware that
he was kissing her forehead and her cheek and her throat,
tender, soothing kisses. His palm stroked her hair over
and over. "Shift just a little, honey," he murmured.

She couldn't seem to obey; she was far too content
as she lay with her cheek in the hollow of his shoulder.
With a smile, he reached over her and dragged his chamois shirt closer, tugging it under her to make a soft nest

for her on the crushed grass. "Better?" he murmured.

"I have no idea," she murmured back.

He smiled again. So very busy he was, stretched out next to her, taking one strand of her hair at a time and lifting it to his shoulders. It took a very long time, yet eventually the entire rest of the world was sealed out by a silvery blond curtain. "I would have waited, Anne," he said quietly. "I would have waited as long as you wanted me to."

Her lashes whispered down on her cheeks. He'd wanted to wait, to show her they had more than sex. She'd hurt him, she knew, when she'd said that. She'd never meant to hurt him. She opened her eyes, needing to tell him exactly what her dark prince had meant to her over the years...not quite able to. They'd filled such a unique, such an oh-so-special niche for each other for so very long that even the word *love* seemed inadequate. What they had was infinitely precious to Anne, as fragile as it was real...but that was not all he was looking for. And she couldn't hurt him again, not now. Her hand stroked his cheek, her palm soft against the afternoon beard that was already starting to roughen his skin. Her limbs felt like butter, yet her heart had already picked up an uneven beat. Despair...out of nowhere.

"You've certainly changed over the years," he said casually. "At eighteen you all but asked me to make love to you, wiggling your hips around in a miniskirt..."

"I beg your pardon." Her eyes flickered wide.

He nodded sadly. "But you've become inhibited, Anne. Particularly since you passed thirty. I mean, look at this..." He plucked a blade of grass from her hair, waving it in front of her nose.

She snatched the offending wisp of grass, her lips fighting the tug of a smile.

"I'm really not sure there's any hope for you," he said thoughtfully. He found another piece of grass and decorated the crevice between her breasts with it. Then another. "You're a sad case. You have no interest in sex, no desire. Honey, it's going to take a lot of work to get you back in shape..."

Her fingers curled in the hair on his chest and pulled. "So you weren't satisfied, Mr. Rivard? You dragged me out here in the middle of nowhere to get grass stains on my bare back—"

"I was perfectly satisfied," he assured her readily. His eyes seared hers and held them a moment. Long enough. "It's you I was worried about," he said quietly.

"You have no need to be worried," she whispered.

"But I am. I am *very* worried." Gently, he pushed her cheek to his chest so he could lean over her, and then he brushed off the bits of ticklish grass and earth that seemed to have molded themselves to her slender back. Three more blades of grass he found in her hair; he showed her all three of them as if he were showing off trophies. "We're going to have to undertake a long reeducation where you're concerned. With constant work and effort, I'm almost certain we'll be able to rekindle *some* kind of sexual feelings in time..."

Anne snatched his hands before he had the chance to find any more trophies, locked them firmly around her waist, and raised her parted lips to his. "Jake," she said gravely, "maybe you could stop talking for a minute and a half and get on with the lesson."

"Now?"

"Now."

He shook his head, his eyes full of laughter. "I have a headache. And besides, I really don't think you fully realize where you are. What kind of behavior is this, lying naked beneath the sun, not a mattress in sight? It's not even night—"

A small pinch on his backside shut him up. A rain of grass on his face, and suddenly they were on their feet, and he was chasing her, a race full of laughter through the meadow with her arms flung wide, embracing the day and the sun and, shortly, the man.

* * *

It was midafternoon, another somnolent, Indian summer day, with a warm breeze just barely lifting the leaves in the distance. Anne stepped out of the motor home with a shallow black pan in her hands, headed toward the stream. In the last three days since she and Jake had made love in the meadow, her appearance had gone through some drastic changes, none more apparent than at the moment.

She was wearing a skirt, a typical Anne tweed, and a delicate blouse with a lace-banded collar. Which was fine, except that the blouse was hanging outside the waistband of her skirt; its sleeves were carelessly rolled up to her elbows; her legs were bare, and on her feet she wore Jake's black boots. Her hair was coiled, but only because long, loose hair would have been constantly in her way. She had tacked the coil in place loosely with tortoiseshell combs and a few pins, but long, free strands fluttered around her face and curled under her chin in the breeze.

Jake, behind her, was laughing.

"We've been here three whole days, and you never once mentioned that your creek runs gold," she scolded over her shoulder.

"I must have told you ninety-nine times. You don't suppose you were preoccupied with other things?"

She would have told him which one of them was preoccupied, except that she nearly slipped as she neared the jumble of wet rocks near the bank of the creek. "Let's get businesslike here," she said absently.

"By all means."

Gingerly, she stepped into the low, rushing stream. The clear water gurgled and danced around the ankles of the huge boots; she could feel the cold—but not the dampness—in her toes. "Ready. Now what do I do?"

He came up from behind her and stood on the creek bank. "First, give us a kiss."

She offered her face up to the sun as he waded into the creek and planted a swift peck on the tip of her nose. Jake just looked at her with that crooked smile of his, then took the pan from her hands and crouched down on his haunches. Anne did likewise, and immediately felt a dozen intimate muscles vibrate; those intimate muscles were feeling just a little sore. A love hangover, she thought ruefully, and changed positions so that she was bending over from the waist next to him.

"Now, before I show you how to pan for gold," Jake said gravely, "I need another kiss."

She shook her head. "You're getting no more kisses, you greedy man. On with it!"

"I must remind you that all you can hope for is about three-tenths of a troy ounce of gold for every ton of sand and gravel you pan. And that this stream has been worked and reworked for over a century—"

"All these irrelevant details," she told the sky disgustedly.

"All right, all right." He dug the pan into the streambed, brought some fine sand up from the bottom, and started swirling it slowly. "It's a question of weight; gold will settle on the bottom because it's heavier than sand. Did you know that any good miner names his placer deposit after a woman? That's a fact. A deposit named for a woman will yield higher dollar value."

"You didn't tell me that, but I'm certainly not surprised." She took the pan from his hands, swirling it the way he did.

"Now, don't look for glitter; that would just be fool's gold. You're looking for yellow—"

She waved him back to his blanket on the grass. Jake could be a terribly distracting man. And then, he'd made merciless fun of her ever since she'd told him she intended to look for gold.

She must have chosen an unfortunate place to begin, as there was neither yellow nor glitter, just brown. Tan-brown sand. A strand of hair dropped in front of her eyes; she whipped it back.

An hour later, she'd tried four different places in the stream; her coil of hair had come completely undone, the hot mountain sun had stolen between her breasts and

was baking her, and she was laughing as she stepped
precariously between stones to get out of the stream.
Jake was stretched out on the soft, grassy bank, leaning
back on his elbows, the sun rinsing a pale yellow in his
hair and giving a pewter luster to his eyes as he watched
her approach. "What have you got this time?"

She dumped her yield on the growing pile next to him,
tossed down the pan, slipped off the boots, and collapsed,
her head in his lap. "I'm exhausted."

"I can see why." Jake respectfully fingered the nugget
she'd brought him, then motioned to the rest. "Quite a
little cache you've accumulated there. A little quartz. A
little sylvanite. A little copper. A lot of just plain rock . . ."

"Plain rock!" she protested, and held one of her trea-
sures to the sun. The gray pebble had a vein of glittery
white, as if someone had etched a picture on it, almost
in the shape of a tree.

"Definitely not plain rock," Jake agreed hastily. He
tugged her up next to him, his shoulder providing a much
better pillow than the unyielding muscles in his thigh.
Anne leaned back contentedly, happier yet when Jake's
face leaned over hers, blocking out the ever-beating sun.

"You're barefoot," he whispered.

"I know that."

He shook his head, his fingers aimlessly trying to
restore order. "Your hair is a terrible mess."

"I know that, too." Jake and immaculate grooming
didn't mesh, not at the intimate level their relationship
had established itself on. One had to make allowances
for a man who thought a silver filigree necklace looked
just as good on bare skin as against a backdrop of expensive fabric.

"You look beautiful, Anne. So very, very lovely . . ."
His finger slowly traced her profile, from her forehead
to her lips. His eyes were suddenly grave on hers, as
grave as she'd ever seen them. "Ready to go back down
that killer road?"

Ready to face some semblance of reality?

Anne shook her head, instantly feeling uncomfortable

pricklings. She wanted to stay here with Jake, making love day and night, eating and laughing with him in their private meadow high in the mountains . . . She wanted to savor every remaining minute of her two weeks with him. At the end of that time— She refused to think about that. Her heart knew only that she wanted to treasure every second, every moment, that she didn't even want to waste time sleeping.

"I've got more to show you," he whispered persuasively. "Some people I want you to meet, and then we'll go to Coeur d'Alene, Anne. I have something very special to show you there."

"Do you have business to take care of?" she inquired carefully. "Because I could stay here, Jake. You can go do whatever you have to do—"

"Nope." He lurched up to a standing position and reached for her hand. "We'll come back here, Anne." He pulled her next to him . . . very close to him, thigh to thigh. "But I'd like to think I can keep my hands off you, for a few hours at least."

Two hours later, as they got into his jeep, Anne looked behind her, memorizing the valley and the stream and the look of the mountains in Jake's ghost town. She had the sudden stricken thought that she would never see it again.

chapter 11

"SHOULDN'T YOU HAVE called them, Jake? It's not polite to drop in on people when they don't know you're coming . . ." Anne smoothed down her skirt, a houndstooth A-line paired with a black short-sleeved cashmere sweater. Her hands were still shaking from the harrowing ride down the mountain. Belted into the jeep, she'd felt as if she were riding on the Ferris wheel at a carnival, only at suicidal speeds.

"Reed and Carla wouldn't know what to do if someone called them ahead of time before dropping in. They're not mere friends, Anne, more like adopted family. Reed was the one who filled me in when I came here, told me everything about the area."

"But what if they're not home?" She snatched her purse and stepped out of the jeep as Jake did.

"It's Thursday night." Jake took her arm as they followed a narrow cobblestone walk. They had left the jeep behind a gas station; there was no other place to park. The narrow streets of Wallace barely allowed room for drivers, much less parking spots, and as she'd already noticed, there was no room to put additional parking space unless it was carved out of a mountainside. "Thursday night?" she echoed back.

"Reed's a big believer in celebrating the day before Friday."

She chuckled, picturing the character of Jake's friend rather clearly. But she still felt a little uncomfortable as they started walking. Three tiers of wood-frame houses climbed the hillside to their left, accessible only by stairs. More than half of them, Jake had already told her, were over a century old. Which was interesting, just as she found the whole town of Wallace interesting, but the feeling of being a fish out of water wouldn't leave her. This was a long way from the world and the people she knew. It wasn't that she was shy of meeting strangers, she told herself, straightening her sweater for the third time. It was just . . . she was shy of meeting strangers. She always had been. There had been too many strangers in her life. Her mothers' husbands, the staff and classmates at each new school . . . "Jake," she said hesitantly.

He stopped on the walk, turning toward her with a smile. Dressed in jeans and a blue-striped shirt, he looked irrepressibly Jake, casual and comfortable no matter what he wore.

"I'm dressed wrong," she said unhappily.

Those shaggy eyebrows of his flickered up, perusing the soft black sweater and impeccable houndstooth skirt. "You look terrific."

"And . . . silly. The thing is, when I packed to come with you—"

His hand curled around hers. "Honey, when you're alone with me, I like you without clothes. When you're with other people, you dress the way you feel comfortable. Your natural style is more formal than mine, which is perfectly fine. Is it any more complicated than that?"

Not when he put it that way, although Anne had the fleeting thought that a fashion designer would blacklist Jake for life. They climbed to the third tier of houses and stopped at the doorway of a tall, dark green two-story house. The man who answered the door had jowls like a basset hound's, big, warm, friendly eyes, a thatch of unruly black-gray hair, and a can of beer in his hand. *"Jake!* I didn't expect you back for another week at least. And you, darlin'—"

"Anne," she supplied, already smiling at the homely, cordial features of the big-shouldered man.

"Anne," he echoed, shooting a stern look at Jake, and threw an arm around her shoulder as he led her inside. *"Carla.* We're getting a divorce!" he shouted to someone in another room.

"How about next Tuesday?" a feminine voice shouted back to him.

He paid no attention, his eyes on Anne as he gave her a bear-type hug. "You're a lot prettier than he ever let on," Jake's friend told her, and leveled another threatening stare over her shoulder. "You *could* have brought her any day but Thursday, when we might have had a chance to get to know her."

"Anne can cope with the crowd," Jake assured him.

Reed took it on himself to ensure that Anne felt comfortable, introducing himself before he rattled off another eight names...eight, nine, ten...of the other people gathered in the two rooms she could see. A beer can was placed in her hand, and just as promptly taken away.

"The *ladies* are having cherry punch," a redheaded wisp of a woman informed Reed. She wiped her hands on a dish towel as she rose up on tiptoe to kiss Jake. Rapidly, she scolded a child for turning the sound too high on a TV set in another room, and then extricated Anne from the bearlike grip of her husband. "I'm Carla, Reed's wife, if you haven't already guessed. Come on into the kitchen with me; you can't enter a whole houseful of strange people and sit down by yourself. Who are you going to talk to? I always feel terrible when I have to do that. Reed, you big oaf, bring her some punch. Oh, wait, maybe you'd rather have beer..."

"Punch is fine," Anne assured her, preferring something nonalcoholic. She added immediately, "But anything is fine."

"That's exactly how I feel when I'm making potato salad," Carla agreed with an impish grin. "I hate making potato salad. For heaven's sake, keep me company..."

The kitchen was no less chaotic than the rest of the comfortable house. Two high school boys with their father's jowls were stomping in the back door, peeking at sealed containers on the crowded counters as they sauntered through. A woman with stern features and a smile of pure sunshine started a second conversation with Anne as Carla continued chattering. Anne caught her name—Alice. Carla placed some deviled eggs in front of her, to be transferred to a serving plate, and tied an apron around her waist. They had shouted down her earlier offers to help, but this just wasn't the kind of household where one could sit on the sidelines and worry about being shy.

Gradually, Anne sorted out what was happening. When Reed's mine was open, he and Carla celebrated Thursdays. The people in the other rooms were their kids and neighbors, miners, people who worked in the town. Two were mining professors from Spokane; another was a doctor. They all seemed to get together regularly once a week. Each guest brought a dish to pass and a six-pack of beer.

"Usually the beer is warm, since my fridge'll only hold so much," Carla admitted. She leveled a worried stare at Anne. "You like the punch? It's a mixture of crushed apples and cherries. I made it myself in the fall, but it doesn't turn out the same way every year."

"It's delicious," Anne said truthfully. The drink was tangy and cool; her throat was parched, and she'd drunk two glasses already.

Dinner was set out haphazardly on the kitchen table, to be collected in equally haphazard fashion and eaten wherever one could find a seat. The menu was simple: ham, potato salad, bright red Jell-O, sweet potatoes in a hickory-nut sauce, chestnut bread. Anne caught a glimpse of Jake an hour later, when he came in to get a plate—and, perhaps, to check up on her. His palm made a circle at the small of her back. "Doing okay?"

"Absolutely fine." Her smile was meant to tell him she didn't need taking care of. She'd seen he was engrossed in a nonstop conversation with one of the mining professors and a burly man she assumed was a miner.

"Anne?"

She glanced up from filling her plate.

"Watch the punch, honey."

She glanced at the table and noticed that the punch bowl was almost empty and that her hostess had her hands full. When she'd found the pitcher in the refrigerator and refilled the bowl, Anne meant to sit next to Jake, but Reed claimed her, steering her to a seat next to him in the already crowded living room.

"He'll talk your ear off," Carla warned Anne. "When you've had enough, just call out for Jake."

"We're going to talk about our divorce," Reed informed his wife.

"Yeah, yeah. You've been promising me that for eighteen years." Carla handed her husband her plate and went to retrieve a sprawling six-year-old from the top of the bookcase. Carla then reclaimed her own dinner and wandered among guests, a bright red bird with ceaseless energy.

"I love that woman," Reed informed Anne.

Anne chuckled as she speared a forkful of food. "Have you two always lived here?"

"Our families have been here four generations. Always the silver... Once it gets in your blood, it's damn hard to get it out." He gestured in Jake's general direction. "He's the exception to the rule. Most times we're friendly people here, but to have someone new arrive and try to settle down as one of us..." He shook his head. "Just doesn't happen. He's nothing like the rest of us, but he still fits in, if you get my meaning. You going to marry him?"

"...Mmmmm," Anne said expressively—savoring the taste of the ham.

Reed nodded to his eldest son, who filled Anne's glass

yet another time with Carla's delightful punch. The room grew increasingly warm; Anne grew increasingly thirsty. Talk finally turned to mining. Anne had the feeling that was inevitable. She settled back next to her host once she'd finished her dinner.

This mine was open; that one just closed; Harvey had been hurt; there had been an explosion and a fire . . . Anne listened, feeling like a foreigner trying to absorb the flavor of their lives. The men lived with real danger day by day in the mines. There was always the chance that a mine would close when the economy shifted or a vein ran out. No one ever considered leaving, though. Even Harvey, who'd been hurt, would stay in the mining community; they would care for him until he was well enough to get a job. These people cared for their own, and had for generations. Their loyalty to one another touched her heart.

Reed kept reaching over to pat her knee. *You're accepted*, said the gesture. He delivered the same proprietary pat periodically to the fanny of his passing six-year-old. The thought made her unexpectedly feel like giggling. Jake had been engrossed for the hour and a half since dinner in a conversation with three men, but he shot her an occasional glance. *Are you still doing all right?* Certainly, certainly, certainly. She felt like laughing again.

"You sure can hold your wine, can't you, sweetheart?" Reed patted her knee yet another time. "I respect a woman who can hold her liquor."

"Me, too," Anne answered blankly, wondering what on earth he was talking about. She hadn't drunk anything but cherry punch . . . but even as a sudden, alarming thought registered, Reed's eldest son was in front of her again, filling her glass to the brim and sending her a twinkling grin. She made a hurried attempt to count exactly how many times she'd seen that twinkling grin . . . when a hiccup erupted from her throat. Anne turned tomato-red.

"I should have known any woman of Jake's could drink 'em under the table," Reed roared in approval.

"Enough of this mining talk. Music, everybody. You have any favorite songs, darlin'?"

"Thousands," Anne agreed brightly. She loved music. From across the room, Jake's pewter-colored eyes suddenly came into focus. He looked distressed. Distressed? She waved a vague reassurance in his direction.

"Rafe and Benjy!" Two men got up to take their fiddles from their cases, with laughter and clapping approval from the rest. "Stand up, honey," Reed ordered her.

Anne obediently stood, for the first time in two hours. Jake's face went out of focus, but that really didn't matter. Everyone was laughing. Laughing and happy. The fiddlers' bows were dancing lightly over the strings.

"You first, darlin'. What do you want to sing?" Reed asked her.

The question made no sense. Anne cleared her throat. "Not sure I understand," she admitted happily.

"We play Round the Horn. All of us get a chance to sing our favorite tune. Doesn't matter what kind of music you like; anything goes. Here, honey." Reed handed her another full glass of Carla's delightfully refreshing cherry punch.

Jake was suddenly, miraculously by her side, apparently having traveled at the speed of light. He intercepted the glass. Anne looked at him in surprise, took her punch back, and leaned contentedly against his shoulder. "Jake wants to sing first," she told Reed, and took another sip of the homemade nectar. Was she really going to have to sing in front of all these people? Normally, the thought would have struck an appalling note of panic in her. Regardless, she was certainly in a mood to hear everyone else. Especially Jake. He was handsome as the very devil, an oddly watchful spark in his eyes for Anne as he took up the challenge, clearly having been through this before.

Leaning back against the edge of the couch, he took Anne with him; an iron hand crept around her waist. Which was nice, because her knees suddenly felt like Jell-O, and being locked between his thighs was not unpleasant. She took just one more sip from her glass before he started to sing. She seemed to have been dying of thirst all evening. In the meantime, Jake's first song fell flat. "Violets for her Furs," an old jazz melody. It failed because no one else could conceivably know the connotation but Anne, and secondly because Jake, sad but true, was tone-deaf. His second song enjoyed a better reception.

It was "She'll Be Coming 'Round the Mountain When She Comes," except that Jake's verse had nothing to do with chicken 'n' dumplings. "She'll be teasing up a tempest when she comes" was how it started—and it deteriorated drastically from there.

These people liked their songs ribald. Lord, they went crazy, stomping their feet and laughing. They were really a hard-drinking bunch, Anne thought vaguely, although Jake, behind her, was still nursing the beer he'd started out with. The man to the left of Jake sang a mountain tune about a nubile young lass. The lyrics turned his wife's ears red; but then, she certainly had a song to match his for lewdness. Carla, the sweet homemaker, came up with a western melody about cowboys and what they did on lonely nights. As each person took a turn, the tunes grew even lustier. The fiddles had everyone's feet stomping.

One by one, around the circle of the room, all of the guests offered songs. Anne's cheeks were flushed from laughter and heat when Reed thumped her shoulder. "Your turn, darlin'."

With her limbs sheer liquid, Anne was not about to spoil the party. But what song did she know of that nature? She handed Jake her empty glass, ignoring the message he was trying to send her with his eyes. She certainly had no intention of letting him down. The old fear that she could never fit into Jake's life...Well, one could get tired of being pegged as inhibited and proper.

This was her chance to change her image. Confidently, she delivered a throaty, sexy rendition of a bawdy old Bessie Smith song.

"Keep on truckin', Mama. Trucking all the whole day long . . ."

Anne threw one hip west, caught in Jake's palm.

"She's the best truck driver this side of town . . ."

She threw the other hip east, crashing again into Jake's opposite palm before she could accomplish the bump-and-grind action she had in mind. She delivered the rest of the song in a breathy roar.

". . . 'Cause she does her truckin' from the hips on down. Keep on truckin', Mama, truckin' all your cares away . . ."

They definitely liked the chorus. Anne was envisioning a singing career, her cheek molded to Jake's shirt. Bessie Smith hadn't been the only one who could belt out a song. Her limp arm extended, Anne accepted pumping handshake after handshake, as Jake moved with her toward the front door. He had one arm tucked under her knees and the other around her waist. Being carried certainly beat walking.

Carla was trailing after them. "Dammit, I'll *kill* him for making her sing. If she doesn't come back here after this because of Reed, he's going to have that divorce he's been joshing me about all these years. Jake, you know he was just trying to make sure she wasn't nervous with a bunch of strangers, that she could be comfortable with this—"

"It's all right," Jake assured Carla.

From about a million miles away. Anne was still humming, tapping out a tune on the second button of Jake's shirt.

"I'm still going to kill him," Carla reiterated with relish.

Who cared? Who really cared? Murder was on the front page of every newspaper. Jake's buttons never rated headlines. Because no one knew, Anne thought sleepily. No one had any idea about the sexy hair on his chest. "Thank you for a wonderful evening, Carla," Anne sang out politely.

"You want an aspirin for her?" Carla asked Jake. "I've got black coffee on the stove . . ."

"Much better than purple coffee," Anne said happily.

Neither Carla nor Jake seemed to be paying her any particular attention. "It's my fault," Carla said. "Everyone who comes in knows the punch is spiked; I should have warned Anne."

"Carla, there isn't a bit of long-term harm done." Over Anne's limp body, Jake and their hostess exchanged a last peck on the cheek. Which struck Anne as terribly funny.

Giggling, she noticed vaguely that the warm, crowded room suddenly turned into a black chill night. Jake's chest drew her like a magnet. She tried to mold herself around that warmth like clay. "Want to make love?" she whispered up to him seductively.

"First, I'd like to negotiate these stairs," he whispered back. "Either you stop squirming or you're going over my shoulder fireman-style."

An idle threat if she'd ever heard one. "I had a wonderful time. I love your friends, Jake. I love Idaho. I love this night. I love . . ."

"Yes?"

Her finger poked his chest. "You never thought I'd sing in front of a bunch of people, did you? Old inhibited, proper Anne. Couldn't strip in front of that hot tub to save my life. I knew what you were thinking—old, boring Anne. I keep waiting for you to be bored . . ."

"I have never"—breathing heavily, he adjusted her 110 pounds in his arms at the bottom of the steps— "*never* been bored with you, sweetheart." He pressed a kiss on her forehead.

"You *do* want to make love," she whispered hoarsely, brimming with satisfaction.

"I just thought I'd take a little on account. Something tells me you'll be breathing fire in the morning."

"Like a dragon, Jake?"

"A dragoness."

That made more sense. She fell asleep.

chapter 12

ANNE WOKE UP to a pair of bright gray eyes leaning over her. Too-bright eyes, and an offensively cheerful smile. She dragged her comforter back over her head, and settled her five-hundred-pound head back into the pillow.

"Now, Anne. I have a nice *plain* piece of toast here for you."

"No, thank you."

"One tiny glass of grapefruit juice, two brewer's yeast tablets . . ."

"God. No, thank you."

"All I want you to do is put a little something in your stomach. Then you can go back to sleep while I drive."

Going to sleep sounded good; grapefruit juice did not. She seemed to be waking up far too fast. Vague, distorted memories from the night before were trying to rush at her. "Did I?" She spoke directly to the comforter. "Jake, if I did anything to embarrass you in front of your friends . . ."

"You don't remember?"

She took a breath. *That* was a mistake. A knife sliced directly into her temples. "I'm sorry. Really sorry," she said unhappily. "Jake, it tasted like fruit juice, and there were so many people that it was hot in there. By the time I realized . . . Carla told me it was homemade, but I thought she meant . . ."

"Excuses, excuses." Jake mercilessly tugged the comforter away from her face. *"There's* my big drinker," he said affectionately, a grin just dying to be let out of the corner of his mouth. "When I tell the lady to watch the punch bowl, she *certainly* watches the punch bowl." He took advantage of her parted lips to nudge a sliver of toast inside. "I really think you should be all upset about this, honey. I mean, it's a terrible habit you've built up. You've had too much to drink exactly once in thirty-one years." His forefinger tapped her nose. "It's just a real shame you don't remember last night, since you had such a good time. You kept most of your clothes on, honestly, you did."

He sauntered up to the driver's seat and started the engine. Anne stared after him. As the engine vibrated to life, she rather hastily realized she had a glass of grapefruit juice in her hand, trying to spill.

She downed it, grimaced, and edged out of the bed. It was no small punishment for the night before, trying to get dressed while Jake drove down Killer Road. They were going to Coeur d'Alene; she applauded herself for remembering that . . .

Jake was humming a vaguely familiar tune when she made her way up to the passenger seat, planning to sit in total silence. The song got to her after a time, though. It was the kind of tune that could drive her crazy trying to remember a title she thought she knew. "What is it?" she asked finally.

"The one you sang last night." He started humming again.

Anne drew an imaginary hat down around her ears and curled up in the seat, her knees tucked up to her chin. The words to the song came to her. All of them. Particularly the chorus.

"And did you belt it out," Jake said admiringly.

"One might be tempted to suggest that you've already gotten your licks in," Anne said politely.

"Reed was ready to divorce Carla for you . . . Reed and the rest of the men there. You know, the guys whose mining stories you were sweet enough to listen to for more than two hours. The women, now, they can appreciate anyone who lets off a little tension from time to time. It's not the easiest life, being married to a miner. Now, if you'd stuck your nose in the air and looked down on them, you'd have had a little problem going back, but as it is . . ." Jake flashed her a crooked smile. "You're invited for the next three thousand Thursdays."

Her conscience knew very well she should be perfectly miserable, mortified, and ashamed of herself. Jake, annoyingly, was making the incident seem unimportant. Despite her reluctance, a small smile tugged at the corner of her lips—never mind her aching head, or a few choice lingering embarrassing memories from the night before. She leaned back, her hair falling in a loose curtain around her shoulders. She'd had no energy to put up the silky tresses, and though she'd managed to tuck a trim cranberry blouse into a gray flannel skirt, she hadn't managed shoes yet. All of which was beginning to add up to irrefutable evidence that she was changing radically.

It was Jake's fault. She *knew* when she'd committed a federal crime in her own eyes. It was *his* eyes that jumbled everything up. Outside the window, fog was settling on the highway, swirling in light gray wisps around the cars. In spite of herself, that small smile kept on coming.

Jake, catching her smile, inadvertently started chuckling. A few moments later, so did Anne. He brought out the worst, the absolute worst, in her . . . but there was no denying Jake was the only man on earth she didn't mind seeing her in that condition.

"Your hips were trying to defy gravity when you really got into the rhythm of the song," Jake told her.

"Isn't the weather nice?"

"And if there's anything else you don't remember

about the evening, I do believe Benjy took a few snap-shots . . . I could get a print or two for you, honey. Maybe blow it up?"

"It's going to be colder than a stone tonight," she said flatly.

"I wouldn't count on that," he murmured.

"Pardon?"

"I said I have a definite cure for your headache, Anne. Just stay strapped in the seat belt for a few more minutes."

Shopping for clothes was his cure for a headache. For miles, the highway out of Wallace held little more than a rugged turnoff for a small mining town here and there, yet suddenly Anne had the sensation of going down, and just as suddenly clouds were put in their proper place. Above her. Not below.

Still, the flash of a long, low blue lake to the left startled her. "Coeur d'Alene Lake," Jake told her, "but we'll get back to the water in a little bit, Anne. First, some civilization for a change."

The city of Coeur d'Alene was a mixture of old and new. A bustling logging industry was centered at one end, and schools and homes and shopping centers nestled high over the lake at the other. Anne found herself staring at Jake as he pulled into a parking lot in front of a row of shops. He certainly hadn't gone out of his way to let her know this kind of gracious living was even remotely close by. Yes, he'd mentioned that he stayed here, but she just assumed the lake meant more camping-out territory. Instead, the schools looked new, and the homes were attractively nestled in hillsides. Trees shaded the streets, and the lake was dotted with graceful sails. Feeling inexplicably lighthearted, Anne fell in step beside Jake as they walked toward the stores. "It's a lovely town," she commented.

"I told you you'd like it. It will be a wonderful place to raise children." He qualified that statement immediately, "Illegitimate children."

Her fingertips suddenly went cold. He hadn't mentioned marriage for days, and now she was afraid he wouldn't let go of the subject again. She stared in rapt fascination at a raw silk suit in the store window ahead of them. The thing's strange stripes of muted orange and purple horrified her. "What do you think?" she asked Jake.

"About your having my children, on any terms you like?"

"I'd like to buy a pair of jeans, but there's no need for you to go inside with me if you don't want to," she said firmly. "I promise you I won't be long..."

She pushed through the revolving door of the next shop. Western wear was its theme. Jeans and cords were piled high on tables, surrounded by buxom mannequins in plaid or flannel shirts. Rapidly, Anne fingered through the nearest pile of cords, paying no attention to size. A shakiness seemed to have infiltrated her nervous system. *Don't push it, Jake...*

"Tell me you don't want children," Jake said determinedly from the doorway. Both saleswomen looked up, and so did another wandering customer. Anne flushed. Jake was standing with his hands loosely on his hips, shoulders flung back, staring directly at her as if no one else existed in the world. There was nothing for it but to cross the room to seize him and drag him back to the pile of jeans...granted that he was willing.

"I have never once told you that I wanted children," she clipped out in a furious whisper.

"But you do."

Through a miracle of fate, she found the size eights. "Every woman who wants children doesn't make a good mother, Jake. Some people probably think they'll be perfectly wonderful, and other women turn out—"

"Like your mother," Jake said flatly. He held up a pair of lobster-red jeans. Anne shook her head with exasperation, but Jake went on, "So that's what scares you. Honey, you couldn't be any less like her. How long have you been fretting about that one? You'll be an outstanding mother, Anne. You'll be there whenever your kids need you, with a cool head and a warm heart, willing to listen, involved and interested..."

She felt something catch in her throat. "I've never had any experience with little ones." He lifted up a pair of turquoise jeans. Anne took his busy hands out of the clothes pile and put them back on his hips, trying to ignore the curious stares they were getting from other people in the store.

"What does experience have to do with anything? I figure by the fiftieth time, if only by chance, you'll get the diapers on straight. Does that kind of thing really matter, anyway? I've never heard that psychologists with Ph.D's in child development raise the happiest children."

Anne gathered up a pair of soft gold cords, then brown ones. Jake reached the shirt racks before she did. "Well?" he demanded.

She draped two shirts over her growing pile, matching flannel plaids to blend with the jeans. "I don't know why we're talking about this."

"Because we have to talk about things that scare you," Jake said reasonably.

Only he wasn't looking reasonable. He had that wolf-ish look again, the sheer male determination stamped in the stark silver of his eyes. Anne was well aware that he really *didn't* care if anyone else was in the store. Or the universe. "Jake, I'm going to try these things on," she said uncomfortably. "I won't be long—"

"I love you, Anne. Would you kindly stop panicking for two and a half seconds?"

One saleswoman put her elbows on the counter and leaned forward to listen, clearly enthralled. She looked from Jake to Anne, evidently expecting a comeback the way she would expect the return of a Ping-Pong ball.

Color stalked up Anne's cheeks. "I love you, too," she whispered back to Jake. "That has nothing to do with anything!"

She pivoted in search of the dressing room, and es-caped promptly behind a coarse white drapery. In seconds, she had stripped off her gray wool skirt and cranberry blouse. Mirrors reflected her oyster satin camisole on three sides; she fumbled for the gold cords and started pulling them on. Before she had them snapped at the waist, the drapes parted, and Jake let himself inside, ignoring her startled gasp.

"Did you mean it?"

"Jake, you're going to get us kicked out of this store!"

"Nonsense, there's almost no one else out there. The saleswomen understood. Did you mean it?"

"Did I mean what?" She snatched up a camel and brown flannel shirt and pulled it on, ten thumbs struggling with the pearl buttons.

"That you love me?"

Her hair got caught in everything, the hair that she had neglected to coil up sensibly that morning. "Conflicting lifestyles and potential divorce are the issues, Jake, and you know it. Not *loving*. You know I've always loved you—"

"No." Jake turned suddenly quiet, ominously quiet, although he shoved aside her hands, efficiently brushed back her hair, and dealt with the buttons himself. "You haven't always loved me. You accused me of acting only on sexual vibrations, but that, sweetheart, was a description of *you*. It was fun in the beginning, Anne. I enjoyed playing the aggressor who came back to storm the fortress and win the lady again—but it was you who let the physical chemistry block out a thousand other feelings ... feelings that mattered. I waited a long time for you to see more, for you to see the man I am. I had a role in your life, but only as lover, Anne—because you didn't want more."

"That's not true. You always took off—"

"And I always asked *you* to come with me."

The shirt was a bit too snug. The jeans were a tad long. She stripped off both shirt and jeans, reaching for a pair of denim pants. She was shaken, and badly. He was her dark prince—she had given him that name, and it wasn't pleasant to be accused of being insensitive to his feelings. Only he wasn't accusing her of anything; his voice was gentle with understanding, and somehow that hurt more. "Jake, it isn't that simple. A woman these days has her own life, her own work. Do you really think it would be easy for me to drop my life and take off on one safari after another?"

"You've got a good head for finance, Anne, but that doesn't mean you're limited to working in a bank. You could be a broker or a CPA. I've been telling you that I need some financial advice, but you haven't helped me at all. You could at least *lift* your wings—even if you don't want to spread them." The last seemed to come out in a mild roar; then Jake changed subjects so smoothly she almost missed the transition. "This outfit looks better. The first blouse pulled under your arms. This one—"

"You don't *really* need my help," she blurted out.

"The hell I don't."

"You know *perfectly well* you made up the whole thing about wanting a trust."

"I don't care what I made up. I need your help."

She drew in the first deep breath she'd taken in several minutes. Jake's critical eye was fastened on the mirror, taking in the pink and tan flannel molded softly over her breasts. The tan cords fit like an Italian kid glove. Unobtrusively, she stole a glance at her rear end in the mirror, and was not overly thrilled at what she saw. "These pants are too tight," she said swiftly.

"They are not."

"Yes, they are."

"Bend over."

Enough was very close to enough. She glared at him.

"Test them out," he said patiently. "Bend over; see what happens."

Nothing remarkable happened. Jake gave a short, boring lecture on the fit of jeans. Anne cut him off in midsentence. "Look. You must know that if I ever thought you *really* needed me, Jake, I would be there. It's not— "

"Good. I do."

The saleswoman was waiting for them with a sassy grin. Anne had the feeling the woman had heard enough to last her the rest of the day, and now Jake was arguing with her over who was going to pay for the outfit . . . at least until he pulled out his wallet.

A sheepish grin came over his face as he glanced up at Anne. "All I have is four dollars and thirty-five cents."

She started chuckling as she paid the bill, and was still chuckling as they drove to the bank. Jake paid for lunch. Corned beef on rye with dill pickles. "We have to get you some shoes," he said abruptly.

"I have tons of shoes."

"Not the kind to wear with jeans."

He purchased ankle-high boots in a soft deerhide, nothing Anne would have chosen for herself in a thousand years. Back in the motor home, she relaxed in the passenger seat and enjoyed the feel of new soft textures next to her skin. Jake kept casting her wayward grins.

Her heart was trying to work itself into a major anxiety attack over the subjects they had broached in the clothing store, but the momentum seemed to be lacking. Jake had dropped the topics like hot potatoes, just as if they had never been mentioned.

After they left Coeur d'Alene, the road wound along the water's edge for miles. Wolf Lodge Bay, Beauty Bay, Gotham Bay, Silver Beach . . . the sparkling blue waters of the endless lake snuggled into coves at every turn. In spots, tall white pines and paper birch hugged the shore. Suddenly there was a row of unique cottages and homes; then red rock cliffs edged right down to the side of the road. The gold leaves of autumn were reflected in the mirror-still surface of the water. Ferns played on the forest floor, turned apricot for the season.

Jake pulled off the lake road and motioned below . . . another private cove, with three spacious homes set far apart on the wooded shores. "What do you think?" he asked her.

Anne had no problem. "Gorgeous."

"Of the three houses, which is your favorite?"

She studied each one, treating the game with mock seriousness. The first was an A-frame with a glass front and a wooden balcony, very trim and attractive. The second was a three-story brick house, narrow and tall, built into the side of a ravine with balconies on all three floors and immaculate landscaping.

The third had forest-green wooden siding and was built low, half on the water, with ceiling-to-floor glass paneling in a huge room that jutted out over the lake. The green house wasn't meticulously landscaped like the others. Sprawling trees and bushes created a privacy that the other houses lacked. A deck extended from the glassed-in room, leading out to a gazebo over the water, and one side of the house held a triangular stained-glass window that caught the sunlight on the lake and sent back rainbows.

"You like the brick one, I'm betting," Jake said.

The more conventional, conservative one. Anne shook her head. "Sorry, Jake, but I can't always fit the mold. It's the green one that draws me—"

He let out a loud, pent-up sigh. "Thank God." He sent her a happy smile. "That one's ours, honey."

Chapter 13

"I'M ALMOST CERTAIN I misheard you," Anne said crisply.

"I've only owned the house for four months, Anne, and haven't had the time to really do much with it. You'll have to see what you want."

Relaxed and easy, Jake parked the motor home not five minutes later. Redwood steps led down the steep slope between the driveway and the house. Jake took them ahead of Anne, pausing only when he realized she was standing in utter shock at the top of the steps. "Don't you want to see it?" he inquired politely.

"Since when have you ever had the least interest in acquiring a house?" she blurted out.

"Never, particularly. I don't really care where I hang my hat. But *you* do, don't you, Anne?"

His words sent a shiver up and down her spine. Her new boots suddenly picked themselves up and took off down the stairs after him. "Jake—"

"The grounds require almost no care. There's no lawn to mow, since the woods lead right up to the beach. That's not the reason I bought the house, though. I couldn't resist that glassed-in room over the lake."

Not the usual motivation for buying a piece of real estate. Head swimming, Anne stepped through the doorway ahead of him.

The house was built in a basic square, with a kitchen island set kitty-corner in the center of the main living area. Its counter faced the glass-enclosed living area. Two low, well-stuffed couches in cantaloupe faced the lake as well as the stone fireplace. Near the hearth was an area that could serve as a living room, although at the moment there wasn't a stick of furniture in it. Off-white carpeting ran through both rooms, thick and springy beneath Anne's feet.

She kept moving, out of the living-dining area toward an open door. The master bedroom was next. Her practical side noted its built-in closets, the king-sized bed and ivory shag bedspread, the need for plants and pictures. Her less practical side kept focusing on the huge, jeweled window. The stained-glass design was a profusion of hyacinths in coral and lilac and ivory. The pastel softness cast a sensual glow of color and shadow on the entire room; Anne could imagine it at dawn and sunset. With her heart racing oddly, she found herself staring, mesmerized . . .

Then she realized Jake was standing at the door. Anne bit her lip, and ducked under his arm. Too many feelings were flooding her mind; she wasn't ready to face them yet. She turned the knob on a closed door and felt Jake's hand clutch at her shirt, plucking her back from a potentially very wet, very cold, most unexpected dunk in the lake. "Our garage," he said wryly.

A boat was bobbing in their "garage." No huge ocean liner, but white and gleaming and large enough for a cabin.

"An absolute necessity," Jake explained. "During Idaho winters, the roads are often impassable with snow around here. The lake's so huge it rarely freezes over, and there are docks in Coeur d'Alene."

"I see," she said faintly, and kept on going.

Beyond his "boat garage" were two spare bedrooms that faced the woods. Both were decorated with nut-brown carpeting and apricot curtains, but they were without furnishings as yet. She found one last room as they finished their tour of the house. It was a study with three long, rectangular windows, half-filled bookcases, an ox-blood leather couch and oak desk complemented by warm paneling and dark blue carpeting. In furnishings and mood, the room was completely different from the rest of the house.

"Your office," Jake mentioned.

Anne's already well-established case of panic went into high gear.

"You're looking pale, honey. I'll get you something to drink."

"Not alcohol," she said swiftly.

"Not alcohol." Jake grinned, her favorite crooked smile. The one that had torn at her heart from the first, so many years ago. "Because they built the kitchen at an angle in the middle of the house, one of the bathrooms on the other side is a triangle. Check it out," he advised as he sauntered off toward the kitchen.

She did. The tub was in one point of the triangle, a sunken affair, large enough for two to stretch out in . . . if both were shaped rather triangularly. Not funny, Anne . . . Melon tiles climbed the walls; gold fixtures reflected back from the mirror. So did Anne, or at least there was some strange woman staring back at her with vulnerable green eyes and a mane of ash-blond hair.

What was he trying to do to her? He hadn't said one word about the house, not when he was trying to convince her to come west with him, not during the three days they spent in his ghost town. She walked out of the bathroom, and turned the corner to find Jake in the open kitchen, holding a cup of peppermint tea out to her. That struck another note of anxiety; so he had stocked peppermint tea. He must have bought it even before the trip. Jake leaned back against the counter as Anne took the warm cup in her hands. He said nothing, as if waiting.

Words struggled out of her dry throat. "This house cost more than a penny here and there."

"A little more coin than that, yes." He made a sweeping gesture. "The whole place needs furniture."

"And pictures."

He nodded. "White carpeting probably isn't particularly practical?"

It was terribly impractical. Anne loved the house, though. All of it, from the gleaming appliances and easy-care surfaces, to its impossible-to-keep-clean white carpeting, to the pastel accents, always favorites of Anne's. She put down the cup and touched cool fingertips to her temples. Her eyes riveted on a tiny patch in the knee of Jake's jeans and couldn't seem to focus anywhere else. She couldn't remember a single time since she'd met him that he hadn't worn patched jeans.

Gradually, she forced her eyes to stop staring. Just as gradually her gaze made its way past the blue cambray shirt, open at the throat, past lips no longer smiling, past that strange nose of his that gave him such a strong profile. Gray eyes met hers, fiercely concentrating on the fragile paleness of her own face. "There are times, Jake," she said in a low voice, "when you scare the hell out of me."

"Then first," he suggested, "we'd better take care of that."

He only had to take a step to reach her, to capture her trembling lips with his own. She was so strangely cold, and then not at all. The warmth of his arms was reassuring, welcomed more than she could tell him. Her hands swept up to his muscle-padded shoulders, as familiar as the taste of him, as the feel of iron thighs rubbing against her own. This *was* Jake, no stranger...

Yet he *was* a stranger. She'd known Jake the lover forever, but, as he himself had said, she'd never known *the man* before. She knew the wildly impulsive lover who could buy out a townful of violets on a whim, who wrapped up silver ingots as a surprise, who could stalk her through a crowded room like a silver wolf without another soul guessing what was going on. No woman could resist the fantasy web of magic Jake could weave—

but how long had Anne equated the fantasy with the total man?

Only now did she realize the different kind of web he'd been spinning day by day. His cactus salad and threat of yellow-jacket soup—how like the Jake she once thought she knew. Now her heart remembered something more, her response to the very strength of the man, the soul of a survivor who knew his way around the wilderness.

His friends, too... They didn't live at all according to her preferred lifestyle, but neither were they leading the here-today-gone-tomorrow lives she'd expected. Stereotypes wouldn't do; they were simply good people, caring people, and the way they cared for Jake had touched her.

His ghost town—and how exotic she'd been afraid that place would be—had turned out to be simply a haven. And his silver—she'd been so sure he'd been taken in by some con artist selling worthless stocks. And last, his house, built half on land, half on water—so like Jake. So very like Jake. Only she was not fooled this time. The house was a clear offer of exactly the kind of security he knew mattered to Anne, and she felt as if he'd spun a cobweb tightly around her like a silken net.

Panic still quickened her pulse, a panic she couldn't explain. She just couldn't make decisions right now, not the decisions he wanted from her. Fear warred with a far more primitive, simpler emotion... the need to be held by him. To be held so close she didn't have to think for a minute. She didn't want to think. It seemed far more desperately important to let him know she saw the man, *loved* the man, not just old images and fantasies. A fierce hunger rushed through her veins as his hands crushed her hair, as his lips brushed hers, over and over. He made the foolish mistake of trying to lift his mouth from hers to take a breath. She wooed his lips back to hers, enticing him with a soft, sweet, murmured plea.

He caught the mood. The hold-me, don't-talk, fierce-sweet mood. Lips clung and tongues tangled and Jake didn't let go. His eyes flickered on hers once, so very gray; she saw his surprise at the woman who'd always savored a softer seduction—surprise...and pleasure, for the uninhibited response she was offering. That instant changed everything for Anne. She forgot her fears, forgot his house, put aside the thought of marriage, life, death, everything. Just Jake mattered. Her breasts played the rub and tease of a Gypsy dance against him; her thigh brushed between his; her fingers whispered over his neck, into his hair. If he wanted her to be aggressive, she would be aggressive. He could have anything he wanted. From her depth of love came his endless choices.

Jake's breathing changed, turned harsh and low. He pulled her flannel shirt free from the waistband of her jeans, his hands stealing inside to find soft flesh...but they didn't find flesh. His fingers splayed over the sexy satin camisole he had bought her.

"I wore it for you," she whispered. "Do you like it?"

"Not," he growled, "at the moment."

She would have smiled if she'd had the chance. She didn't. His lips sealed hers as he lifted her high, his tongue still savoring all the sweetness of her mouth. They were going to bump into walls on the way to the bedroom, she knew that. Jake certainly wasn't paying any attention to where they were going. And she couldn't seem to raise any interest in opening her eyes. Her hands were feverishly trying to undo his shirt buttons—which refused to cooperate. The throb of his heartbeat beneath her palm seemed to announce the start of something—a race, perhaps. A terribly important race in midafternoon with the sun so lazily beating down on the still waters of the lake. His house was totally silent except for the sound of Jake's breathing as he set her down next to the shaggy white spread in his room, as his hands chased the shirt down from her shoulders. She was busy with his own, finally understanding why his buttons wouldn't give—they were western snaps. One ruthless tug and they obediently pulled apart. The sound of that snap-snap-snap in their quiet house...Jake gently nudged up her chin with his thumb.

She saw the sensual fire in his eyes, his suddenly roguish grin.

"I don't know what on earth you think you're doing to me, but I like it," he murmured. "In the meantime, who punched the fire alarm?"

Anne kissed him quiet, smile matched to smile on their lips. He was such a very foolish man at times. Why on earth would anyone have punched a fire alarm when the whole world was welcome to burn down?

They could have undressed a great deal faster if they'd taken off their own clothes, but they didn't. They slipped off each other's shoes, then socks. Arms and wrists crisscrossed in an effort to immediately undo each other's belts and buttons and zippers. Very low whispered laughter came from nowhere. Anne's cords made a puddle on the floor, then Jake's. The race only slackened because of the triangular window.

She'd forgotten it, but now she saw the colors shimmering on Jake's golden flesh, the luminous hues dancing in her hair, in his. When Jake moved to touch her, his whole body seemed liquid in motion, a kaleidoscope of fluid coral and light purple. Fascinated, she watched his hands as they slowly reached to touch the spot above her heart. Her breasts, too, looked jeweled. It was like crossing over to a magical world.

From rampant speed to slow motion, their moods had changed. So slowly Jake unlaced the front ties of the camisole. As he slipped down the straps, the fabric slowly parted to reveal firm, creamy soft breasts, proud nipples flaunted for him, her bareness displayed in patterns of diamond and silver-lilac and coral. The garment slid to her feet; he again lifted her high.

"Look at you," he whispered. "Look at you, love..."

She was looking at *him,* aware of the texture of the shaggy spread when he laid her down, aware he was taking off the last of his clothes, but interested far more in the look of color and shadow on his skin. He was a beautiful man. Sinew more than muscle, a grace that was pure male, a pride he didn't know he even had, every time he moved. And he was always in motion. His head was at her breast, his lips seeking first one nipple, then the other. Their peaks turned rigid for him. The look of his brown hand next to her so-white flesh sent lightning, long jagged streaks of it, flashing through her bloodstream. His hand traced the soft flesh of her stomach and then traveled lower, evoking an unconscious cry from Anne.

He inhaled that sound, in a kiss that left her breathless. A languid, sensual weakness was trying to steal over her limbs, a memory of Jake's power as seducer... but that was not what she wanted for him, not this day. She shifted away from him, just slightly. Her fingertip traced slowly down, burrowing in the hair on his chest, pausing to circle the pebble of flat male nipple. On down, to explore a flat, hollow navel, hidden in silver-wiry hair. His pelvic bone, she traced all of it...

His whole body went taut. His hand found hers, drawing it back to her side as he leaned over her. Dark, luminous eyes seared her own. *What is it you want?*

For you to lie still. This was new for her, playing the role of aggressor. It was new, the depth and confusion of love she felt for Jake; she needed to express it. She could feel those silver eyes watching her, but he was silent. He watched her flick back the errant strands of long hair. Her fingers danced over his skin, then rubbed, then teased again with lightness. Her lips followed. Her need was to please him, and she forgot that he was watching. Her long, silky hair—he'd always loved it. She took a handful and gently brushed the strands over his chest, down his stomach, lower still to much more intimate flesh, taking an incredibly long time...

From nowhere, she found herself flat on her back again, her eyes filled with a rainbow of stained-glass prisms, all reflected on Jake's face. "Honey, give me credit for the patience of a saint," he murmured.

"No one would suggest you were a saint," she began on a husky murmur.

"This time, yes. Oh, yes, Anne. But no more..."

He took her with the light still dancing on them, the afternoon sun still so delightfully pouring through the windows. When light gave way to late-afternoon dusk, they napped. But when it was dark, moonlight played through the stained-glass window, and they were again caught up in the magic of the senses. Jake played the slow torturer this time, a role he had always assumed expertly. But Anne was learning.

The next day was busy and the next, and the next. Anne had a long list of things to accomplish—unpack the motor home, put away the food, vacuum and scour the vehicle, buy groceries, wash clothes, whisk away the thin layer of dust in Jake's house...

Jake had an equally long list of priorities. A long walk through the woods behind his house, a boat excursion on the lake, lunch in the gazebo over the water. His list was longer than Anne's. He had a lot of odd hours scheduled for more critical activities: laughing, making love.

On Wednesday, a storm whipped up on the lake around noon, distracting both of them. Lightning pierced the frothing water in sizzling yellow slashes, casting a fluorescent glow on the surrounding trees. Branches shook and swayed in a mad dance, and thunder roared out huge, angry bellows that seemed to surround the house. The clear, still waters of the lake turned wild, and if Jake's arms hadn't been around her, the vision from Jake's glass-paneled living room would have been close to terrifying.

They watched for an hour, until nature's fireworks settled down to a steady, pelting rain. They turned to each other then, Jake with a rueful smile for the day's plans gone awry. "No walk today," he said wryly.

Anne had to agree. And she couldn't have been less eager to do household chores, either. "A good book," she suggested.

"And hot cider with cinnamon sticks."

They holed up in the study, Anne at one end of the couch and Jake at the other. After a great deal of fussing, they got their legs tucked together properly, rested their warm mugs of cider on their chests, and opened up their respective books. *The New Money Dynamics* for Anne, a Mickey Spillane novel for Jake. They chuckled at each other's idea of a good book, and then both heads bent down.

Anne tired first, setting down her mug to stare absently at the oak desk. Papers had begun to pile up there since they'd arrived. It seemed this was to be *their* office. The look of never-serious rogue didn't fool Anne anymore, though Jake had obviously scheduled a total vacation for himself these few weeks, although he'd made more than a few business calls when he thought she wasn't looking. Anne didn't let on that she noticed. The man she was so restlessly, so totally, frighteningly in love with didn't want her to think he had anything on his mind but her.

Unfortunately, that made her love him more.

Unconsciously she found herself studying him, the beak nose and sun-weathered skin, the silvery sideburns that truthfully needed a trim, the way his brows arched downward in concentration. Her eyes softened helplessly, the longer she looked at him.

There was a small corner in her head that was still holding out on Jake; she couldn't explain why. The dozens of things that had always made a permanent relationship with Jake impossible... many of them he had dispelled. The house—she knew it was for her, a measure of his knowing how much she valued security. And if his involvement with silver still struck uneasy chords, she could not deny his serious attitude toward it. This was no fly-by-night venture for him; he knew what he was doing. Coeur d'Alene was a perfectly lovely place to raise children...

Several times, she nearly interrupted whatever they were doing to tell him she wasn't going home at the end of the week. Yet she hadn't. She knew she loved him; a fool couldn't doubt he loved her. But there was something, a restless, ceaseless worry in the back of her head, at the very center of her heart.

How long would he really want to settle down? Would he be happy in the same place, playing father and husband just like other men? Could cautious Anne, hung up on stability and schedules, really hold his interest for the long term?

His eyes flickered to hers, and she hurriedly opened her book again. To the same page she'd already read four times. Jake's stockinged toe suddenly started a lazy circular motion on her hip. Her palm enclosed his toes scoldingly. He chuckled.

"You're bored with that book," he accused.

"I am not."

"You are. When are you going to amble over to the desk and sort out my mess?"

She flipped the page. "You don't make a mess. You just keep on with that theme because you know it makes me worry about you." Narrowed eyes scolded him over the top of her book. "A typical masculine ploy."

"How could you misjudge me so terribly?" He sounded wounded.

She plied a fingernail down the length of his foot, and chuckled when he laughed. They read for another moment or two, until Jake said casually, "The IRS is going to do an audit on me next month."

Every muscle in Anne's body went instantly rigid.

chapter 14

LIKE A GENERAL facing Code Red, Anne's mind registered *Emergency* with frightening efficiency. Jake smiled at her lazily. The next five minutes were a mass of confusion. Jake opened up four paneled doors, revealing built-in drawers and cabinets, boxes of tumbling papers. Anne raced to the kitchen to make coffee. Desk drawers opened and slammed; Anne adjusted the light above the desk.

The noise abruptly ended. Jake returned to his Mickey Spillane adventure, occasionally rising long enough to refill the coffee cup on her desk. The storm ended in late afternoon, and dusk settled in with total calm. When Jake brought in a tray of sandwiches and set it on the carpet, Anne rose from behind the desk for the first time in two and a half hours. She settled cross-legged on the floor, across the tray from Jake, vaguely aware that two weeks ago she would never have considered picnicking on the carpet when there were perfectly good tables strewn throughout the house. An irrelevant thought.

Jake handed her a sandwich, a huge amalgamation of ham and bacon and turkey and lettuce and cheese, so thick she could barely get her fingers around it. "So what do you think?" he asked casually.

"That it would take an efficiency expert *months* to get you organized." Green eyes made every attempt to cow the humor in his own. "Have you ever heard of the word *file?*"

"Sure."

"I don't believe it. Spell it."

"F-i-l-e," he obliged. He swallowed a mouthful of sandwich, not easy to do when he was wearing his widest crooked grin. "The lady is about to spit a little fire," he speculated to thin air.

"Don't be ridiculous. Just because you've stuffed receipts in shoe boxes? Just because you've got active bank books buried in a mound of candy wrappers?" She took a sip of tea. "Did it ever vaguely occur to you that when you fill out your tax returns in crayon, the IRS might get a little curious?"

"Now, Anne. Let's not exaggerate."

"No one overpays the IRS one year by some ridiculous sum, and then the next year turns in a half-done tax return with a big check and a note that says, 'I'm sure this will cover it.'" Her voice was rising in spite of herself.

"I was busy last year at tax time." He brushed the crumbs from his hands, his silvery eyes glinting on hers, full of amusement, and certainly not concerned. "Why does everyone see the IRS as some kind of enemy? I don't care if they come here and turn everything topsy-turvy. What's the difference? I've got nothing to hide."

She cradled her head in her hands. "Just bring me an aspirin, would you?"

He sighed, his expression turning serious as he pushed the tray aside. "Anne, in certain ways, I know well I'm probably not going to change. When I take on something, it's for the challenge of it, not the money involved. I like to earn money, but once that's done, the challenge is gone. Hear me?"

"All I hear is that you have to be the first person in history to get in trouble with the government for overpaying your taxes," she moaned distractedly. "Jake, hasn't anyone ever mentioned to you that people cheat right and left to get *out* of paying taxes? Do you realize exactly how much you've thrown away by never acquiring a tax shelter?"

"But that's all your bailiwick," he said patiently, and drew her up to a standing position. "Come on, time to clear away the cobwebs. Let's sit outside."

Jake took the tray to the kitchen, then draped a sweater over her shoulders as they wandered outdoors, making their way to the narrow wet dock that led to the gazebo over the water. The storm had left the lake unbelievably calm and clear; stars shimmered on the surface like diamonds on black velvet. Waves lapped gently at the shore, reminding Anne of the sleepy rhythm of a lullaby.

Jake's gazebo was five-sided, with two sides walled for privacy and shade and the others screened for a clear view of their cove and the lake. Two chairs were wet, but the lounger, tucked in the shaded corner, was dry. Jake stretched out first, then pulled Anne between his thighs. She leaned back, resting her head on his chest, her pulse beating at a still-troubled rate—but less so. No matter how concerned she was for his finances, she had also just spent hours bent over a desk, and this break was welcome. Jake crossed his arms under her breasts, comfortably secure. "Now do you believe I need you?" he asked finally. "Things have rather gotten out of hand the last few years. The silver boomeranged on me; I had more profits coming in than I ever expected. And my trip to Tulsa just seemed to be a case of being in the right place at the right time. Actually, Anne, the money started accumulating when I was still a kid, fishing off the coast of Alaska. I had nowhere to spend the money while I was stuck on that boat. It just sort of all got away from me . . ."

Unfortunately, she could believe him. Not that anything had "gotten away from him," but that he honestly hadn't noticed how much wealth he had accumulated over the years. Jake really just didn't care about money;

he never had. His fingertips gently combed back her hair, and Anne sighed in confusion. Even that casual touch was a whispered call to another world: sensual, primitive, dark. Filled only with Jake. "Normal people hire accountants," she tried one last time, but there was no bite left in her voice.

His lips hovered at her temples. "I know my tax accounts wouldn't be a full-time job for you, Anne, but there's more than enough financial work around here to keep you busy the rest of the time. I never expected that you would be happy just sitting home. Maybe with children, in time . . . but that will be up to you. And Coeur d'Alene has possibilities for you that we haven't even talked about."

For a man discussing career possibilities, his hands were certainly on a different wavelength. He shifted her so she was lying at an angle across his lap, her head tilted back in the crease of his shoulder. In the darkness, shadows and light played over his features, making his silver eyes glow as they came closer. "I *need* you, Anne," he whispered. "The way you argue, because you're so darned pragmatic and so intelligent, your warmth and your laughter and the way you fit next to me. The sound of your voice. I need your heart—"

"You have it, Jake. You've always had it," she murmured.

He shook his head. "A part, never all. I want *all* of you, honey."

Those smooth, cool lips settled over hers—but they weren't at all cool now. Warmth and tenderness were so much a part of his kiss that a ripple of sheer sensual tension rocked Anne. Heart, body, soul . . . was that all he wanted? All of them at that precise moment went on the auction block. Her tongue slipped inside his mouth, wantonly wooing him, teasing the tip of her tongue against his.

Her hands were busy pushing aside his shirt, seeking the crisp hair on his chest, the feel of his flesh. Jake broke off the kiss with a low, vibrant sound from his throat, and lifted her up to pull off her green cashmere sweater. Night air touched her skin, raised prickles of sensual awareness along her flesh.

His eyes wouldn't leave her own, as if he sensed that something was different. She couldn't have said herself what sparked the change in feeling. She had been totally exasperated as she worked over his books, not frustrated with the figures so much as with the man himself. Jake, so darned different from her—salt and pepper... and she'd always known that. But the word *need* had spiraled something irreversible, something that reached the soft core of her, which no one had ever touched. Hers was the need, need for the only other human being who could fill her heart, create feelings of richness and a joy in just breathing.

She ached with those feelings now, longed for the simple right to touch his skin, the right to hear the rasped intake of breath as she stroked the long, tight muscle in his thigh. She felt as if she were absorbing him, inch by inch, cell by cell. Her lips pressed into the hair on his chest, seeking first his heartbeat and then trailing over to his flat nipple, where her tongue reached out and nudged the male bud to hardness.

Slowly, her lips trailed back up, to the underside of his chin, all bristly with a night beard. *"Anne."* She was wearing a skirt that day, for no particular reason that she'd discovered until now. His hand was sweeping long, slow caresses up her stockinged leg, stealing very slowly underneath the skirt fabric. His palm on the curve of her thigh, molding up and over her bottom, ignited a fire in her loins, a sparking, brilliant, bright orange fire. His chin nudged at hers. "We're out in the open," he said with a harshness that almost made her laugh.

"It's a dark night, and there hasn't been a boat out since before the storm," she answered.

"You're beginning to sound like me. That's terrifying."

"You don't look terrified," she said impishly.

He nipped at her neck. "I hate to tell you this, honey,

but there is no possible way to make love on a chaise longue."

She reached for his belt buckle and undid it. There was enough leeway for her fingers to slip inside the waistband of his cords. His stomach flesh was exquisitely sensitive. Her finger could touch his pelvic bone, trace it quite a little distance. "Oh, well," she murmured. "If we can't, we can't."

Within moments, the chaise mattress was spread out on the redwood deck. Clothes were draped over chairs. And Jake, very rapidly, was draped over Anne. His body surged forward to join with hers, with exactly the fevered speed she craved . . . and then stopped. Locked inside her, he rested his weight on his elbows, staring down at her with glowing, brilliant eyes. No smile touched his lips, but there was a softness . . . "You're staying," he whispered, only half a question.

"Is the offer still open?"

"Don't be light, Anne, not about this."

Her eyes unaccountably filled—for the vulnerability she heard in his voice, for the aching swell of love inside her. "I want to, Jake," she said simply.

Her words seemed to call forth a tidal wave. A long, passion-induced frenzy washed over her, born of Jake's hands, Jake's mouth, Jake's exquisite feel and motion in the core of her. The water splish-splashed beneath them as they were swamped and drowned and reborn, over and over like a tumbling mystery of nature, wild and primitive and soaring with the joy of life . . . and loving.

Anne's laughter echoed throatily as Jake pushed the glass doors closed behind them. "That's certainly the first time I've ever streaked," she said mischievously.

They were both carrying bundles of their clothes, and shivering just slightly because of the run from dock to door. "Get a robe on, Lady Godiva. And be thankful it's past midnight and every light is off around the lake." Jake's eyes flickered first to the clock on the wall in the kitchen, then back to Anne's bare limbs and the stream of ash-gold hair swaying almost irresistibly to the curve of her bottom. "I'm hungry," he announced suddenly.

"So what else is new?"

His slash of a grin was accompanied by a teasing palm on her backside. "I was *talking* about a nice, juicy steak."

"That's not where your eyes were looking." She picked up Jake's shirt and pulled it on, but his fingers nudged hers aside to do up the two buttons he wanted, leaving a disastrous amount of cleavage showing and her hair tucked inside. Flicking back the cuffs, she was humorously aware that the look was not going to sell to a fashion magazine, but she glanced up and saw that Jake didn't seem to agree.

"You have unbelievably perfect legs," he mentioned solemnly.

"You just want me to cook your steak." Anne, too, glanced at the clock. "You will undoubtedly have dreadful dreams if you insist on eating at this hour."

He shook his head. "I've always had a cast-iron stomach."

Moving past him to open the refrigerator, Anne murmured absently, "That isn't the only part of you that tends toward cast iron."

Jake was leaning over the counter when she turned to him with a defrosted steak in her hands. "What was that you said?"

Heat flooded her cheeks. "How do you want your steak?"

But he took it from her hands and got out the broiling pan. "I'll cook it. Sure you don't want one?"

"No, thanks."

But the delectable aroma that soon wafted from the broiler made her change her mind—as far as hunger was concerned. She poured some soup into a pan and punched the button for simmer. While they were both waiting for their respective midnight feasts, her eyes wandered absently to the counter. Stacks of mail had arrived for Jake that morning; he'd opened and skimmed over the stuff but left it. A brochure with a picture of a coffee bean on its cover caught her eye.

"I've been interested in coffee for ages," Jake admitted. "Did you know that in Tokyo, they have health spas where the people put on paper bikinis and get buried to the neck in dry-ground coffee? It's supposed to be therapeutic."

"There's a lot of rumbling these days about how dangerous coffee can be," Anne commented.

"Exactly. And being a morning coffee-aholic myself, I got intrigued. Almost to the point of journeying to Colombia...or maybe Indonesia. The industry's worked hard at options—taking out the caffeine, taking out the acid—but a lot of people still insist that coffee is a health hazard. Obviously, the thing to do is go to the coffee plant itself, and all kinds of experiments are being tried. People want their morning coffee, but there's money to be made out there if someone could guarantee that the potential dangers were taken out of it."

Anne shivered suddenly, as if an ice cube had just been run up her spine. Jake served her soup and then pulled his steak from the broiler with pot holders. They settled next to each other at the counter and started eating like starving fools. Her strange sensation of being chilled disappeared as they chattered, more nonsense than sense, although by the time she began to wash their few dishes, Jake was rambling on about another interest of his.

The Silicon Valley in California...computer chips ...sixteen-billion-dollar worldwide semiconductor market...the valley's need to keep the competitive lead in the endless trade war with Japan...

Anne curled up in the fold of Jake's arm on the couch, sharing one last glass of warm cider before sleep. Listening, she could have lazily shaken Jake for all the years when he had never offered one word as to his own interests, beyond a brusque, lazy statement of where he'd been and what adventures he'd been up to. She loved hearing the sound of his voice, and she loved discovering new depths to the man. Jake put months of study into anything he was even minimally interested in, simply for the joy and challenge of it. Anne felt sleepy and loved and enfolded in the cloak of sharing . . .

But the chills kept coming, from the very depth of her heart, from the most vulnerable corner of her being. She asked questions and smiled and curled closer . . . and all of that was real. Just as real as the wrenching cold inside her that kept growing.

"Bed," Jake announced finally, and stretched as he got off the couch, reaching out a hand for her.

She took it. His fingers securely held hers, familiar and warm. In the bedroom, they slipped out of their clothes, and moments later were curled together spoon-fashion. Jake was half asleep almost before his head hit the pillow, but Anne's eyes flickered open.

She had to ask, her voice lazy and sleepy and studiedly casual. "So you're losing interest in silver, Jake? You think you'll move on to coffee soon? Or to the Silicon Valley?"

Jake's voice, like Anne's, sounded sleepy. "I can't imagine ever completely losing interest in silver. But as far as what comes next . . ." He leaned over in the darkness to kiss her forehead. "I don't know, Anne. There are still a thousand things to do out there. Does it really matter?"

"No, of course not." She closed her eyes, snuggling against him, feigning sleep until she heard his even breathing. There was no other answer she could have given him. She'd made a very real commitment of love. And just as she knew Jake would try to move mountains to make her happy, she also knew his soul would never be content in one place for long—but she'd known that when she made the commitment.

Still, her *no* seemed to echo in the darkness, like the whispered cry of a child from a long time ago.

chapter 15

DREAMS HAUNTED ANNE'S SLEEP. First, of packing her
dolls in a suitcase. "You'll like him, Anne," said her
mother. "Really you will." She had; but her stepfather
hadn't liked her. Locked in a closet for an offense she
could no longer remember, she felt suffocated by the
yawning darkness; her lungs were desperate for breath
despite her low keening whispers. Her terror was too
great to cry out. The door opened to light that hurt her
eyes. "Oh, my God," her mother said.

Packing again. Boarding school. The ache of loneliness that never left, hugging books to her chest for comfort . . . then packing again. Another wedding, the smell
of champagne floating like a wisp in the dream, then the
sip she'd sneaked. Another strange house, and another
and another; they all rushed past her in the dream. Packing again, packing again. "You'll like it here, Anne.
Really you will."

A puppy was wrenched from her arms, and suddenly
she was older, with budding breasts encased in a stiff
white blouse and wearing a Black Watch plaid skirt that

was too long. Her grandmother was standing in front of her, stiff and proud and proper; no one cried in front of Jennie; no one would dare. "I want to stay with you," Anne said quietly. "Please don't send me away. Please . . ." She didn't cry. A maid took away the worn blue suitcases. Anne never saw them again.

A foggy cloud surrounded the image of a tiny boy in the dream. Jake's child, with big, vulnerable gray eyes and a crooked smile and shaggy, blondish hair. "You'll like the new place," Anne told him. "Really you will." And she got out a big blue suitcase and looked around for Jake in the dream. Only Jake wasn't there, and suddenly Anne was crying . . .

Her lashes fluttered open. The bed was empty beside her. Sunlight shone gently on the king-sized bed and thick white carpet, all with a soft coral cast from the stained-glass window. Disoriented, Anne closed her eyes for a moment. There was a lump in her throat; she couldn't seem to swallow properly.

"You're finally awake, sleepyhead?" Jake's head appeared at the door with his most mischievous grin. She couldn't seem to look at him and stared blankly at the tray in his hands instead. "Peppermint tea," he announced. "Toast. One omelet, à la Rivard. What's wrong, love?" A sharp gaze pierced the hollows under her eyes.

"Nothing." She tried to smile. "I just didn't sleep very well."

"Breakfast will perk you up."

"It looks delicious." She pushed the pillow behind her, still somehow unable to look at him. "You're a master at spoiling me, Jake," she scolded, and hoped her voice had just the right amount of teasing. The normal amount.

"You need spoiling," he answered, but there was something in his voice that time that wasn't normal. The grave, harsh note made her eyes flicker up to his . . . and quickly away.

She tried to do justice to his breakfast—really tried.

Perhaps if Jake had tried to make conversation... but Jake suddenly didn't seem interested in small talk. She felt like a moth pinned on a slide under a microscope. He was watching her. She could feel his eyes—inside, outside, all over.

He took the tray when she rose to get dressed. Not even thinking, she found herself taking up old modes of dress, a camel skirt and long-sleeved navy silk blouse, austerely tailored. She made up her face and wound her hair in a sleek, efficient coil. The old perfection faced her briefly in the bathroom mirror; she didn't look at it long. Her heart was ripping itself into shreds.

Going back into the bedroom, she found Jake walking toward the closet. He glanced at her appearance, his face oddly expressionless, strangely without color. He pulled an old denim jacket from a hanger and put it on.

"Jake—"

The words were clipped. "I don't want to hear."

She swallowed, sick inside. "It's not that I..." she started, then stopped. He'd crossed to the dresser, and was shoving his wallet into the back pocket of his jeans. *"Jake.* I just want a little time to think. I..."

She was talking to thin air. He'd left the room. She caught up with him in the kitchen, where he was taking a key from the hook by the stove.

"Listen to me," she said desperately. "Jake, I fell in love with your Idaho and your silver and your house and even your crazy ghost town. But I thought you were telling me something else. I thought you were telling me that you'd finally found something important enough to you that you'd want to... *settle* ... somewhere. *Anywhere.* In the desert, the jungle, the mountains. I love *you,* not the place, but—"

The door didn't slam in her face. Actually, it closed very, very quietly. She heard the sound of the motor-home engine, and in another minute there was silence. A terrible, terrible silence.

Was it suddenly forty below? Anne wrapped her arms around her chest, shivering violently. Tears filled her eyes. He hadn't even pretended to listen, she thought furiously.

Worse than that, she had a terrifying suspicion that he wouldn't be back. This was his house, of course; he had to come back to take care of it sometime. In a thousand years. Jake didn't care about the house. He'd never cared about houses.

The knowledge of desertion seared through her like a knife. Old scars opened for the blade. She knew exactly what desertion felt like. Her mother had changed loyalties so readily; her father had died; people had passed in and out of her life so often. She knew far better than to count on living people. Jake alone had always been there for her.

Only Jake...

Tears gushed into her eyes as she wandered through the empty rooms. Oh, you *fool, you fool.* So fast, so painfully fast, the old scars ripped open. How long had she equated security with the wrong things? Jake had *always* been there for her.

And you let him *go?* The finality of that door closing echoed in her ears. How could you, how could you, how could you... Frantically, she wrenched open the door... but Jake had taken the motor home. The jeep was still in the Silver Valley. The boat, which she didn't know how to operate anyway, wouldn't take her anywhere except around the lake.

She fumbled for the phone book in a drawer in the kitchen. *Too late, too late, too late.* She dialed the number of a car-rental agency. Yes, it had cars available— if she could get there to pick one up. She could hardly walk all the way to Coeur d'Alene. How *dare* he just leave her like that? Dammit, he'd rushed her every step of the way: was it so inconceivable that she just might need the chance to think for two minutes and realize what a total idiot she'd been?

A neighbor a half-mile down the road drove her to the car-rental agency. Mrs. Barker, a big-boned woman in purple shorts, was clearly not used to opening her door to a woman with hair streaming down her back, crying her eyes out. In the next life, Anne would undoubtedly remember that taxis existed. In the next life, perhaps, so would Mrs. Barker. In this one, one woman simply reacted to the panicked, incoherent pleas of another woman.

The rental agency offered Anne a Mustang with a stick shift, for the money she had in her pocket. Anne stopped crying. She had an hour's shopping to do in Coeur d'Alene. Florists' shops, but then Anne wasn't thinking clearly. The back seat was filled with her purchases by the time she set off on Highway 90. There was no question where she was going. The airport at Spokane would have been the prudent choice. Jake had clearly written her off. Anne was only beginning to understand that in his own way he'd waited for her from the time she was eighteen, and had waited far long enough. If she was going to get bogged down with those kind of details, though, she would certainly start crying again.

Actually, she did, as she drove east toward the Silver Valley. It was two in the afternoon when she drove through Wallace. She hadn't eaten since breakfast. Tears were streaming from her eyes; and sun poured through the windshield as she reached Killer Road. The first wild uphill curve made her sick to her stomach. Her hands gripped the steering wheel, wet and clammy, as she made the impossible curves and turns, downshifting, then gearing up, panicking on the downhill curves, terrified when the engine balked at the steep inclines.

She didn't question where she was going, because if Jake wasn't at the ghost town, she wouldn't know where to find him. She had to find him. She *had* to find him . . .

Her heartbeat slowed down to normal as she took the last curve and turned off the road onto the gravel lane. Vaulting out of the car, she opened the gate, drove through, and closed it behind her. The sign still said No Trespassing. Which made her start crying again.

When she saw the motor home in the valley, she slowed the Mustang down, stopped. A strange kind of silence seemed to rush through her heart. No one was around. The ghost town was the same. Wind whispered through the firs and aspens; sunlight beamed through the fluttering gold leaves; the stream picked up prisms of color and danced them back for her eyes. Biting her lip to hold back the tears, she got out of the car, pushed the front seat forward, and reached into the back.

The scent of daffodils filled her nostrils, as sweet and intoxicating as a spring breeze. The fragile yellow blossoms were starting to wilt, but the scent was still there, surrounding her as she walked toward the motor home with her arms filled.

She didn't knock, primarily because she didn't have the courage. Opening the door was an incredible effort all by itself; her fingers were freezing cold, almost numb. And a thousand other things had gone wrong. Her hair was wind-tossed from the ride; she knew her face looked white and strained. And she couldn't breathe; there was the most ridiculous huge knot in her throat...

Jake turned at the sound of the door. A coffee cup sat on the counter; he was standing in front of it. Something was terribly wrong with his face; it looked gray, not like Jake's face at all. And his beautiful eyes were cold, the color of stone. There was nothing in his eyes— not shock, not welcome. Not... anything.

Rage, the last emotion she felt, was the only one she could cope with. Trembling, she hurled the entire armload of flowers in his direction. *"Everyone* is entitled to a moment of panic now and then," she told him furiously. "That doesn't mean you just *walk out* and scare someone to death. Don't you *ever* do that to me again, Jake!"

She whirled and stalked out of the motor home toward the car, moving too fast to think, stumbling, not caring. She scooped up the second armload of daffodils, brought them in, and pelted Jake with the flowers one by one. "If you think I care whether we live in Colombia or on the dark side of the moon, you're a fool. If you think our children will care, you're just that much more of a fool. Fools inevitably get their priorities mixed up. It's *different* with us, Jake—how *could* you have been so stupid? We count on each other. What on earth is the matter with you? Some people have never had anyone to count on, but that's not *us*. How could you be such an idiot?"

She ran out of flowers and threw her hands up in the air. "The kids'll have us to hold on to and each other to hold on to and that's exactly what the difference is. I don't know what on earth's been the matter with you all this time that you couldn't see it! Sometimes you can be scared of something for so long that you can't see the forest for the trees. Who cares? It's about time you changed, Mr. Rivard! Because when you've found *love*, the kind of love worth holding on to, you'd darned well better *hold on to it!*"

He hadn't moved. He didn't move.

For that century of an instant, Anne didn't move either, and then her toes moved on springs again, bursting out of the motor home for the second time. Moisture was forming beneath her eyelids again. These tears were very different, as soft and helpless as they were inevitable. *You're just making a fool of yourself.* She stalked back to the car and clasped the last of the flowers to her chest, dropping some of them and breaking the stems of others. She picked up each one so very carefully and then gathered them tightly to her chest so that more stems broke; stems she didn't see. She walked back one last time into the motor home, not looking at Jake, unable to look at him this time. She looked instead at the incredible sweet-scented mess she'd made.

Flowers were everywhere. Broken stems and crushed petals. Jake's shoes were covered in daffodils. One was hanging from his shoulder.

Anne lifted her chin, pretending there were no tears in her eyes. "I'm disgusted," she said flatly. "Totally disgusted. What on earth is wrong with a town that doesn't stock more daffodils? So they're out of season. That's no excuse. Some people manage to buy violets when they're out of season..."

Her voice trailed off jaggedly. She just couldn't keep up the act any longer. Through blurred vision, she finally found the courage to look at Jake. He was still standing by the counter, all but buried in daffodils, setting down his coffee cup after taking a sip. Taking a sip of coffee? *Now?* And his face no longer had that grayish cast to it. "I do love you, Anne," he said mildly, "but it took you a hell of a long time to get here."

She could have killed him.

There wasn't time. In the blink of an eyelash, he had his arms around her and was lifting her high in a crushing rib-breaking hug. She was the one holding on so very, very hard. "You're home, Anne," he said vibrantly.

She was. Home. Not to a place, but to her mate. Security was where love was. Roots were where the heart set them down.

His lips hovered over hers for an instant, and then moved in. That kiss . . . she could smell the heady fragrance of spring all around them, taste all the sweet heat of a languid summer, hear the sensual crackle of leaves in autumn, feel the warmth of his arms around her on a cold winter's day. Let the seasons come and go. As long as Jake was here . . .

WONDERFUL ROMANCE NEWS!

Do you know about the exciting SECOND CHANCE AT LOVE/TO HAVE AND TO HOLD newsletter? Are you on our *free* mailing list? If reading all about your favorite authors, getting sneak previews of their latest releases, and being filled in on all the latest happenings and events in the romance world sound good to you, then you'll love our SECOND CHANCE AT LOVE and TO HAVE AND TO HOLD Romance News.

If you'd like to be added to our mailing list, just fill out the coupon below and send it in…and we'll send you your *free* newsletter every three months — hot off the press.

☐ *Yes, I would like to receive your free*
   SECOND CHANCE AT LOVE/TO HAVE
   AND TO HOLD newsletter.

Name _____

Address _____

City _____ **State/Zip** _____

Please return this coupon to:

Berkley Publishing
200 Madison Avenue, New York, New York 10016
Att: Rebecca Kaufman

HERE'S WHAT READERS ARE SAYING ABOUT

Second Chance at Love®

"I think your books are great. I love to read them, as does my family."
—*P. C., Milford, MA**

"Your books are some of the best romances I've read."
—*M. B., Zeeland, MI**

"SECOND CHANCE AT LOVE is my favorite line of romance novels."
—*L. B., Springfield, VA**

"I think SECOND CHANCE AT LOVE books are terrific. I married my 'Second Chance' over 15 years ago. I truly believe love is lovelier the second time around!"
—*P. P., Houston, TX**

"I enjoy your books tremendously."
—*I. S., Bayonne, NJ**

"I love your books and read them all the time. Keep them coming—they're just great."
—*G. L., Brookfield, CT**

"SECOND CHANCE AT LOVE books are definitely the best!"
—*D. P., Wabash, IN**

*Name and address available upon request